I0598655

Coasts of Christmas Past
From the Tales of Dan Coast

By: Rodney Riesel

Published by Island Holiday Publishing

East Greenbush, NY

ISBN: 978-0-9894877-3-3

First Edition

Special thanks to:

Pamela Guerriere

Kevin Cook

Cover Design by:

Connie Fitsik

To learn about my other books friend me at

https://www.facebook.com/rodneyriesel

For Mom & Dad

KEY LARGO

ISLAMORADA

MARATHON

BIG PINE KEY &
THE LOWER KEYS

KEY WEST

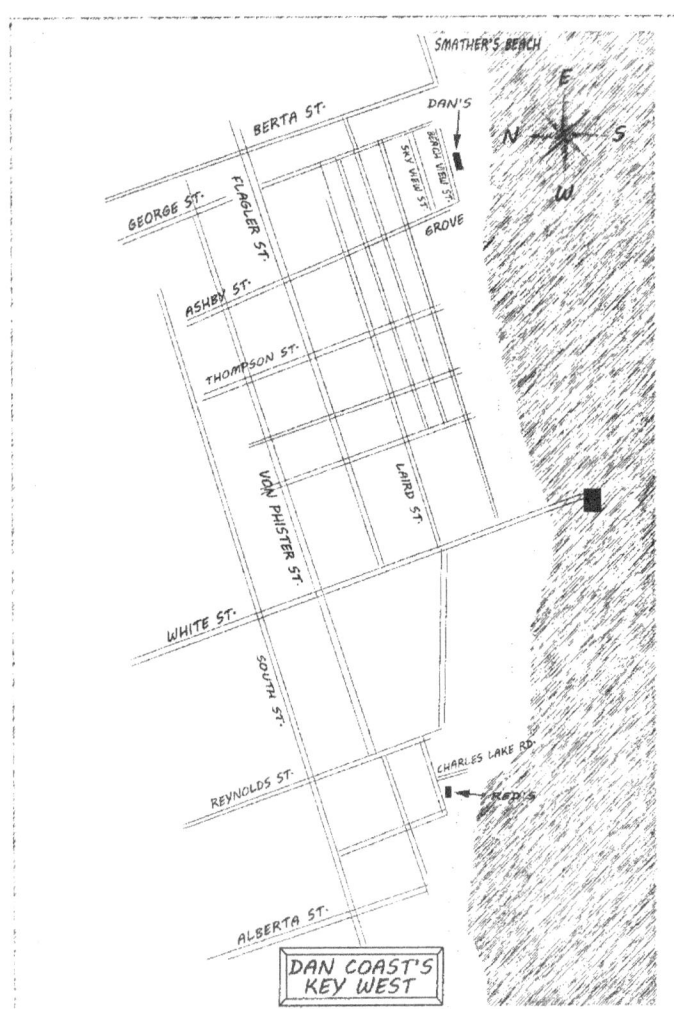

Chapter One

Dan Coast finished wrapping the Christmas lights around the blue spruce that stood in the living room in front of a large bay window. He had started at the top of the tree, and after winding them around and around, he was now kneeling at the bottom on a red and white tree skirt.

The television was tuned to the Hallmark Channel and one of the seemingly endless supply of syrupy Christmas movies starring Ed Asner was playing, and Dan loved every last one of them. A fireplace with a gas insert burned at the other end of the room. The lights in the room were dimmed just enough to appreciate the cozy glow of the fire.

Alex stood over Dan holding a white porcelain angel with a white satin gown. She stared into the angel's eyes. She knew it had seen every Christmas Dan and Dan had spent together. She remembered buying it at a Christmas shop in Cooperstown a few weeks before their first Christmas together.

With a slight groan Dan got to his feet, took the angel

from Alex and looked at it. "I don't think I would have a smile that big if I was going to spend the next five weeks of my life with a pine tree shoved up my ass."

"That gets a little funnier every year," Alex responded with a slight roll of her eyes.

"Hey, what would Christmas be without the classics?"

"Quieter, probably."

"Funny," Dan said as he placed the angel atop the tree and then plugged in the lights.

The tree came alive. There were two strings of colored lights that blinked off and on and two strings of constant on white lights. There were a few glass bulbs hanging from branches but mostly the tree was decorated with various unique ornaments that the couple had purchased on vacations and in little shops here and there. There was a glass bulb with the Yankees logo that had been picked up in the gift shop at Yankee Stadium. There was a yodeling pickle that was purchased at a Christmas shop in Myrtle Beach. There was even a mini Elvis that stood on a platform next to a palm tree and, when you pressed the button, sang "Blue Christmas" until you were sick of it, which for Dan was never.

Alex had spent years trying to convince Dan that a themed tree with matching bulbs would be much prettier, but Christmas was Dan's holiday and Alex knew it, so she never pushed too hard for the change.

"Perfect," Alex said as she turned and exited the living room. "I'll be right back."

Dan picked up his tequila and 7UP off the end table, took a sip, and walked over to the bay window. He set his drink in the window and then adjusted the blanket of cottony fake snow that lay under the porcelain houses that filled the seat board. He reached down and plugged in the cord that powered the lights in the houses. He stared at the houses and imagined it would be a nice town to live in. *A town of eternal Christmas*, he thought, *what could be better?*

Christmas had always been Dan's favorite time of the year. Every year about half way through October he would begin playing Christmas carols in the car and at home. If it were up to Dan, he would have played them all year round, but the yearly requests from Alex postponed them until October. She liked Christmas too, but not the way Dan did.

Alex returned to the living room, her arms filled with packages. She placed the gifts around the tree. "Did you want to put any presents around the tree?" she asked grinning.

"Umm … yeah. I … uh … I'll bring them down later."

Dan *had* already bought Alex's gifts, but he liked to pretend that he hadn't yet. He liked making her think that he was going to wait until the last minute. It was tradition; he knew they were bought; she probably knew they were bought, but they played the game every year anyway. Besides, he knew if he brought the gifts down too early that she would be shaking them and squeezing them and trying to guess what was in each package. Dan on the other hand liked surprises. The packages could have sat there forever and he would never have tried to guess.

Taking Dan's hand, Alex said, "Let's walk out front and see how it looks through the window."

Together they walked out the front door, across the sidewalk and into the street. They stood holding hands facing their house. Big fluffy snowflakes fell from the sky and a light dusting sugared the ground. Dan tilted his head back and stuck out his tongue, trying to catch a snowflake. He caught one and looked to Alex for approval. She was looking at the front window, mesmerized by the pretty scene. He shrugged.

The tree and the little porcelain houses lit up the window like a scene from a Hallmark card. Dan put his arm around Alex's waist and pulled her close to him. She leaned her head against his shoulder and he kissed the top of her head.

"Perfect," Alex whispered.

Dan squeezed her tight. "Yeah, perfect."

*****

"Mister … hey mister!"

Lying on his back in the dirt, Dan Coast slowly opened his eyes and stared up at the blue sky. He could feel the warm morning sun on his face. His arms were stretched out at his sides. In his right hand was an empty bottle of Jose Cuervo. He turned his head and looked at the bottle. His eyes were slow to focus. He turned his head back toward the sky and was startled by the small young boy standing over him.

I don't think we're in Kansas anymore, he thought.

"Get the hell out of my yard," Dan grumbled.

"But this is my yard, mister," the boy returned.

With a groan Dan sat up and looked around trying to regain his bearings. He let out a belch and rubbed his eyes.

"Where am I?" he asked the boy.

"I already told you. You're in my yard."

Dan shook his head and winced from the pain. "What street is this, smartass?"

"Sky View."

Not bad. Only one street off, Dan thought.

"My name is Noah," said the boy.

"Good for you," Dan replied as he struggled to his knees and then to his feet and started walking in the direction of his own home. He didn't know exactly what time he had stopped drinking but he knew it wasn't too long ago because he was still pretty drunk.

Dan made it to the edge of the yard, when he stopped and turned around. The small boy was still watching him.

Dan stared at the boy. Noah had short legs and short arms. His hands were small and his head was larger than normal. He had a thick head of black hair. He was wearing a small blue Hawaiian shirt. The tan cargo shorts looked like full length pants on the boy. On his feet were dark brown flip flops. Dan looked down at his own feet. One of his flip-flops was missing.

"You see my other shoe?" he asked the boy.

"That dog carried it away."

"What dog?"

"There was a black dog laying next to you. When I came out he walked away."

"My names Dan."

"Good for you," the boy said, turning and walking back to his house.

Dan watched as the boy slowly struggled to grab the railing and climb the steps. When he reached the screen door he grabbed a small knob that was fastened below the real door knob and pulled the door open. Noah paused and looked back through the screen at Dan. Dan nodded his head. Noah went in and let the screen door slam behind him.

When the door closed Dan noticed that the knob Noah had grabbed was actually an old wooden thread spool screwed to the screen door. *Necessity is the mother of invention.*

Dan turned and as he made his way across the street he heard a woman's voice call out. "Noah, what have I told you about letting that door slam?" Dan rolled his eyes, remembering how many times he had heard his own mother yell that same phrase, and staggered toward home.

Chapter Two

Dan had taken a short cut through the yard of the house that sat directly behind Edna McGee's. Edna was a widow that lived across the street from Dan. As he walked through her well-manicured backyard, weaving in and out of the hibiscus and croton bushes, and down her concrete driveway, he looked back toward her front window. As always Edna had the curtain pulled to one side, her bony fingers sticking through the sheer panel, and was looking out her window. Nothing got past her. Edna raised her hand to wave but Dan quickly turned his head and pretended not to notice her, and started across the street.

As Dan made it to the middle of the street, he paused to watch his neighbor, Bev. She had just finished hanging a Christmas wreath on her front door and when she finished hanging it she stepped back off her steps to admire her handy work. She smiled. Feeling as though she was being watched, she turned toward the street to see Dan Coast standing there in what, at first glance, looked like a zombie costume. His sallow face was caked with sand, his long arms dangled ape-like at his sides, his clothes were rumpled and dirty and his hair looked like it had been combed with a Weed Eater.

"You look like shit," she called out.

Dan looked down at himself and realized he was still holding the empty tequila bottle. His hands trembled. He looked back to Bev but remained silent. He could feel his body swaying slightly. His mouth was dry and the entire neighborhood spun when he closed his eyes.

"Starting early I see," Bev said.

Dan looked down at the empty tequila bottle again. His head was spinning. He started walking toward his house again. He had made it almost to the edge of the street when he couldn't fight the nausea any longer and emptied the entire contents of his stomach in the street. When he had finished throwing up he wiped his chin with the back of his hand and looked back at Bev. Her nose was crinkled up as though she had just smelled something awful. She said nothing.

Bev watched as Dan staggered up his walkway. He paused for a moment when he noticed his missing flip-flop lying in his driveway. He then proceeded to his front screen door and went in. He looked down at the welcome mat that read THE COASTS. "The Coasts," he whispered as he went through the front door.

Once inside Dan locked the door behind him and tossed the empty bottle on his chair. It hit with a bounce and ended up on the floor. He looked toward Buddy's bed. As usual it was empty. His eyes went to the picture of Alex that sat on the table next to Buddy's bed. He stared for a while, shook his head, and then slowly made his way to the bathroom.

Dan stood at his bathroom sink staring into the mirror. He could hear Christmas carols coming from Bev's house. Perry Como was singing "I'll be Home for Christmas." What a smooth voice, the perfect voice for Christmas. In another life, Dan had always thought he should be called *Merry* Como, in another life.

Coasts of Christmas Past

"No one's coming home for Christmas," Dan said to himself.

He opened his medicine chest and looked through its contents. There was the usual; toothbrush, toothpaste, a comb, shaving cream, Q-tips. Sitting next to a stick of Old Spice deodorant was a prescription bottle. Dan picked it up and read the label: *Percoset, take one pill every four hours as needed.*

Dan fumbled with the, not quite drunkard proof, lid, removed it, and dropped it into the sink. He poured the entire contents of the bottle into the palm of his hand. He counted the pills, about thirty. He closed his hand and carried the pills with him to the dining room where he grabbed a bottle of rum off of the bar, took it with him to his recliner and sat down. He placed the rum bottle between his legs and twisted off the top.

He sat for a while staring into the blank screen of the television and then opened his hand and took the pills. He washed them down with a big gulp of the rum and then placed the bottle back between his legs. He looked to his wrist for the watch that wasn't there, grinned and then looked to the picture of Alex. He picked up the remote control off of the end table and turned on the TV. He flipped through the channels till he came to an old episode of *Magnum PI* and set the remote back on the table.

Reaching down, he pulled the lever to recline his chair, put his head back and got comfortable. He took another big swig of his rum as he sat listening to Magnum and Higgins go on and on about damage that had been done to Master Robin's Ferrari. He closed his eyes and thought of his sweet Alex. With any luck, he would see her again soon.

Dan heard the squeak of his screen door as it opened behind him and rolled his eyes. *Goddammit, what lousy timing!* Then he heard a gabble of voices coming from his front porch. *What the Christ?* He leaned forward and put the footrest down and got out of his chair. Through the window he saw his visitors.

Dan gulped. "Holy jumping Jesus," he whispered in a panic and ran hunched over, out of sight, for the bathroom.

Dan dropped to his knees in front of the toilet.

There was a knock at the door.

He shoved his finger down his throat.

Another knock.

Dan gagged, and choked on his finger.

"Hello—?" a woman called out.

Dan puked up the rum and the handful of pills. He quickly got to his feet and turned on the cold water. Cupping his hands, he filled them with the cool water and splashed it on his face. He did it once more and then rinsed out his mouth and spit into the sink. The shock of cold water to his face and the even greater shock of seeing just who was at the front door seemed to instantly sober Dan up.

Dan took one more look in the mirror and then headed for the front door to greet his guests. He unlocked the door and pulled it open.

"Merry Christmas, Danny," sang his mother. She was grinning from ear to ear.

His father let out a loud, "Ho ho ho," as he pushed past his wife to be the first one to give Dan a hug. "Long time no see, Sonny."

Gene, Dan's father was an aged, heavier copy of Dan. When you looked at the two there was no doubt that they were father and son. Ten years ago Dan and his father were the same height but in recent years Dan had noticed that his father had shrunk to about an inch shorter. The two men's build was almost the same with the exception being, Gene's belly was larger and his shoulders were smaller and rounder. Gene had a full head of gray hair slicked back and trained to stay that way with the help of a jumbo size can of Aqua-Net hair spray. He had recently traded his work boots for a pair of Sketchers sneakers and always wore jeans and a T-shirt, and flannel shirt if it was cold. Gene was a retired self-employed contractor. He still worked; the retired part just meant that he had cut his work week down to about thirty hours.

"Are ya surprised?" Mother asked.

"Oh … I'm surprised all right," Dan confessed.

As soon as Dan's father released his grip on him, Mother quickly moved in for her hug. "Phew, you smell like a brewery," she said, pulling back and fanning the air with her hand.

Peg, Dan's mom, was about five-four. She had battleship gray hair coiffed in short tight curls that, together with her petite stature and laughing eyes, lent her an elfin air. Dan noticed right away that she was thinner than the last time he saw her. He hoped that the weight loss was planned and wasn't the reason why they were here. She was wearing green slacks, a white short sleeved top, a light cream-colored cardigan, and white sneakers. Peg's uniform was always the same but the colors varied from day to day.

"A brewery smells like beer, Mother, I smell like a distillery," Dan corrected her.

"Starting early?" Gene asked.

"Going late," Dan replied.

"Atta boy. How about making one for your old man?"

"It's only ten thirty," protested Peg.

"It's five o'clock somewhere, eh Sonny?"

Dan grinned and went for the bar.

"That's great, we've only been here for five minutes and you two are starting already," Mother huffed.

"Sounds like *she's* the one starting," Gene said, nodding toward Mother. His shoulders shook as he laughed at his own humor. He could see Dan's shoulders were shaking too.

Mother picked up her suitcase and headed for the guest room, shaking her head. "I'm gonna lay down. I'm tired."

Dan walked back to the living room, grinning and handed his father the drink. "Whiskey and ginger ale."

Dan's father seized the glass in his big meaty paw, took a hearty gulp, and let out a satisfied, "Ahh, I needed that."

"Long train ride?" Dan asked.

"Too long."

"I don't know why you two don't fly down."

"She hates to fly."

"Ya know they have drugs for that now."

"Ah, I don't mind the train ride," father said, waving his hand and downing the last of his drink. "Besides," he whispered, "there's this hot babe, Ally, that works at the car rental place in Miami. Looks like a porn star."

Dan grinned. "And I thought you got off the train in Miami because it was cheaper."

"You have breakfast?" Gene asked.

"No."

"Why don't we grab some vittles while your mother is napping?"

"Sounds good. I'll jump in the shower quick."

Dan turned to walk down the hallway when from behind him he heard his father quietly say, "Sonny."

Dan turned around. "Yeah, Dad?"

"We didn't interrupt anything did we? I mean … you didn't have any big plans for the week or so, did you?"

Dan stared at his father for a few seconds. He saw concern in his father's usually jovial eyes. "No, Dad. As a matter of fact I had no plans for the future at all."

Gene sat down in the recliner, put his drink on the end table and leaned back. "I'll watch me some Magnum while you're in the shower," he said as he stretched out his legs and clasped his fingers behind his head.

"I'll wake you when I'm out of the shower," Dan said, knowing full well his father rarely made it through more than ten minutes of any television show.

Chapter Three

"Dad … Dad," Dan whispered.

"Huh?" Gene opened his eyes, his fingers still wrapped around the glass of ice as the condensation formed a wet spot on his pants.

"You ready?"

"Sure. Let me run in and pee first." Gene stretched and pulled himself out of the recliner with a groan. Dan wanted to grab his arm and help, but resisted.

The two men walked out Dan's front door and down the steps. Bev was back in her front yard putting up Christmas decorations. She was on her tip-toes on the third rung of a green fiberglass step ladder, her arms out stretched. She was putting lights around a front window. Bev wore white shorts and the muscles in her legs were tight. The small of her back was exposed. Gene did a double take.

"That looks real nice, Bev," Gene called out, "… and the decorations look good too."

Dan shook his head.

"Hey, Gene, ya old flirt," Bev called back, grinning. "What brings you down to our little piece of paradise?"

"Just a little R&R."

"Where's Peg?"

"I killed her."

Dan shot him a reproving look. "Dad! Jesus Christ."

"Just kidding. She's taking a little nap," Gene said.

"Tell her to stop over later."

"Will do," Gene replied with a wave and a chuckle.

Dan climbed into his beat up, dark blue 2006 Porsche 911 Carrera convertible and started the engine. Gene pulled at the passenger side door handle with a grunt.

"Still broken, Dad."

Gene rolled his eyes and climbed over the door. "Why in hell don't you get yourself a new car?"

"I like this car, Dad."

"I did too, when it was new, but I think its best days are behind it."

"I know how it feels."

"You know how tough it is for a seventy-year-old man to climb over a door like that?" Gene complained as he fastened his seat belt.

"You're better at it than Red," Dan laughed.

"How's ole Red doin'?"

"Good, Dad."

"You should give him a quick call and see if he wants to join us for breakfast."

"I can do that," Dan said, pulling his cell phone from his shorts. He tapped the contacts icon and hit Red's name.

"Aloha," came Red's gravelly voice from the other end.

"Aloha? Let me guess, that asshole next door is playing his ukulele again?" Dan responded.

"You got it, pal."

"I'm on my way to your house now. Have you had your breakfast yet?"

"No, I haven't. Get here as quick as you can. I gotta get the hell out of this madhouse."

Dan and his father pulled on to Thompson Street a few minutes later. Red was sitting on a brick flower box next to his sidewalk with his hands over his ears and his elbows resting on his knees. Dan parked his car half in the street and half on Red's lawn, facing the wrong direction, and shut off the engine.

Red looked up and with a big grin and said, "Hey, Gene old buddy! When did you get into town?"

"Just this morning."

Red got to his feet to shake Gene's hand. "Dan never mentioned you were coming."

"We never told him. We wanted to surprise him," Gene laughed.

"Were ya surprised, Dan," Red asked.

"Oh, I was surprised alright."

Gene turned his head toward the house next door. "What the Christ is that noise?"

"My neighbor," Red sighed.

"Should we go over and check on him? I think Don Ho might be shoving a screech owl up his ass."

"I think he's getting *better*," Dan put in.

Red looked to Dan's two-seater sitting in his front yard. "We better take my car. We're not all going to fit in that heap of shit."

"Heap of shit?" Dan grumbled. "No appreciation for the classics."

The three men walked around the side of the house to the driveway. Gene stopped dead in his tracks and let loose a belly laugh. "A pink Volkswagen Bug?"

"It's only temporary," Red replied sheepishly.

"Yeah, if six months is temporary," Dan said, laughing.

Gene walked around the back of the Bug to the passenger side and looked down at the bumper sticker. "Mafia Wife?" he chuckled.

"Previous owner," Red said.

Dan climbed into the back seat and Gene got into the passenger seat.

"Ya know, neither one of you two boys ever seem to have a girlfriend, and now one of you is driving around in a pink car," Gene wryly observed. "People are gonna start talkin."

Chapter Four

Dan, Red, and Gene sat at a square red table in a turquoise room overlooking the water. The exposed rafters were painted to match the walls. Hanging from the rafters were nets, lobster traps, and other nautical-themed items. On the walls were pictures of lighthouses and old sailing ships. The floor was white ceramic tile with matching grout. Dan and Red chatted as Gene scanned the room like all tourists do.

When the busboy had finished pouring water, the waiter arrived at the table.

"Good morning, gentlemen. How are you today?"

"Just wonderful, pardner," Gene chimed in. "And how are you?"

"I, too, am wonderful, sir. Can I get coffee for you gentle— Daniel! Is that you?"

Startled, Dan looked up from his menu. "Michael," he said dully as he recollected the face.

"You remembered!" Michael cried with joy and began filling their coffee cups.

"How could I possibly forget?" Dan's voice was barely a whisper.

Red and Gene stared from Dan to Michael and then back again, as though watching a tennis match.

"What's it been, almost a year?" Michael asked.

"About that."

"You were working on that missing person case, I believe. Mrs. Garvey wasn't it?"

"Yes, it was."

"I read about you in the paper a few days later. I told everyone I knew that we were good friends."

Red and Gene traded a curious glance. Dan tried not to wince. "So, I take it you're not at the Atlantic Inn anymore?" he said mock politely.

"Yes, I'm still there. I just help out a friend here one or two days a week. The tips are fantastic, and I get to keep up on all the local gossip."

"I'll have the tall stack with two eggs, potatoes, sausage, and two eggs scrambled," Red butted in.

Michael shot Red a snotty look and jotted the order down in his guest pad. "And what can I get for you, Daniel?"

"I'll have the two eggs over medium with toast and bacon."

Michael wrote it down and then looked to Gene. "And judging from the resemblance this handsome young man must be your brother. Am I right, Daniel?"

"He's actually my father."

"Married?" Michael chirped.

"Yes," Gene answered, adding hastily: "Happily."

"And where is your lovely bride this morning?"

"I killed her."

Michael gasped and his hand went to his chest.

"Dad! She's back at my place taking, a nap, Michael."

Red laughed out loud. Other customers looked over. Michael nervously grinned.

"I'll have two eggs over medium, toast, and potatoes," Gene said, chuckling.

Michael disappeared into the kitchen.

"Why do you always have to say that, Dad?"

"Because it's funny," Gene said, motioning toward a laughing Red. "See?"

"Anything for a laugh, right, Dad?" Dan returned, shaking his head, his lips pursed.

"Yeah, wonder where *you* got it from?" Red asked Dan.

"Shut up, Red," Dan responded.

Michael returned a little while later with the three men's orders. Gene slid his coffee cup toward the edge of the table.

"Can you warm me up?" he said.

"Gladly, handsome," Michael said with a wink, filled his cup, and sashayed to another table to do the same.

Red raised his eyebrows and looked from Michael to Gene and then to Dan. When Michael had flitted out of earshot he smirked and shook his head. "Like father, like son."

Gene gave Red's arm a good-natured sock. "Hey, I'm not the one driving around in a pink car."

Dan chuckled.

"Ya got me there," Red said, sliding his chair away from the table. "I gotta use the head."

Gene downed the last of his coffee, and he and Dan rose from the table as Michael returned and handed Dan the guest check. Gene tried to grab the check. "I'll get it," he exclaimed.

"I got it, Dad," said Dan, eluding Gene's flying fingers with practiced ease. His dad was always trying to pay the check. Dan reached into his pocket for his money clip, counted out fifty dollars, and handed it to Michael. "Everything was great."

"Thank you, Daniel. I'll get your change."

"No, that's fine, you keep the rest."

"Thank you very much, Daniel." Michael looked to Gene. "You come back and see us again real soon, Killer," Michael winked.

Gene threw his hands in the air and protested, "That whole killing my wife thing was just a joke," he laughed. "I haven't killed anyone in years."

Michael smiled. "That's good. I wouldn't want them to blame that shooting this morning on you."

Dan cocked his head and lowered his eyebrows. "What shooting?"

"Oh, you didn't hear?" Michael's right hand went to his chest as his other hand went to his hip. "Some guy was shot over on Riviera Avenue this morning. I'm not one to spread rumors, but they say it was a drug deal gone bad."

"Is the guy dead?" Gene asked.

"No." Michael pointed a limp wrist toward a woman leaving the restaurant. "That woman there is a nurse over at the hospital," he whispered. "She said the gentleman was alive but they don't expect him to live. But you didn't hear that from me."

Amused, Gene turned a pretend key upon his pursed lips and whispered back, "Tick a lock! Mums the word."

"Did they get the shooter?" Dan asked.

"No. From what I hear, they found drugs in the victim's truck. The cops think the … shooter, as you call him, was trying to buy drugs from the other gentleman but something must have gone terribly wrong. But you didn't he—"

"I know," Dan jumped in. "We didn't hear it from you."

"That's right, Daniel."

Gene and Dan headed for the door just as Red exited the restroom.

Red waved his hand in front of his nose. "I wouldn't go in there if I was you."

Gene, who had thought about using the facilities, quickly changed his mind. "I'll wait till we get home."

Chapter Five

Dan pulled his Porsche into the driveway of his one story, white with green shutters beach bungalow at 632 Beach View Street. Dan opened the car door and climbed out as Gene hoisted himself over the other door.

"Gene, I'm over here!" Peg called out.

Gene slowly spun around a full three 360 degrees trying to figure out exactly where his wife's voice was coming from.

"Dad, she's next door," Dan said, pointing toward Bev's house.

"Grab us a drink, Sonny. I'll head over and see what your mother is up to."

Dan did as he was told and went toward his front door. Gene sucked in his gut and made his way toward Bev's.

"What are you two ladies up to?" Gene asked as he reached Bev's front yard.

Bev's house was very similar to Dan's. It was a two bedroom, one story bungalow. The rooms inside were set up the same, although Bev's kitchen and bathroom had been remodeled in the last six or seven years. She had no porch on the front of her house, just steps, and she had a back deck that Dan had recently built for her. Bev's house was light gray with dark blue shutters. The front yard was naked but for one scraggly palm tree and one humongous croton bush. A gravel walkway went from her front steps to the street and was lined on both sides with blue flowering plumbago shrubs.

Peg answered, "I saw Bev out here decorating and I thought I would give her a hand."

Bev put the last staple into the window frame she was wrapping with multi-colored lights and then stepped back to admire her work. "There!" she exclaimed as she picked up the end of the light strand and plugged it in. "Perfect." She went up the steps and opened the door, reached around and flipped on the switch. Nothing happened. She flipped it off and then back on. Still nothing. "Shit."

Gene reached into his front shirt pocket and pulled out a small yellow device with two black wires protruding from one end. He walked over, unplugged the lights, and slid the electrical tester into the outlet. The small LED light did not illuminate as it was supposed to.

"Hit the switch off and on again," Gene said.

Bev complied but there was still no light.

"Huh, not getting any power to the outlet. I'll check the box and see if there's a breaker tripped. If not, I'll check the switch."

"Dad, you're on vacation," Dan groused, walking up behind him and handing him his drink.

Gene took a sip. "Well, Sonny, I can't just sit around for two weeks and do nothing."

Two weeks? Dan thought. He downed his entire drink

in one large gulp.

Peg fussed with two plastic snowmen, one large and one small. "Oh, he's fine, Danny," she said. "It will give him something to do. Besides, Bev, it won't do for your festive decorations not to light up, now will it?"

"I can run a cord out the window," Bev suggested.

Peg patted her arm warmly. "No, no, just let him do his thing."

Gene reached down and pulled the tester out of the outlet and returned it to its place in his shirt pocket.

Bev asked, "You always carry one of those with you, Gene?"

"Wouldn't leave home without it."

"Humph! I'm surprised he's not wearing his measuring tape and utility knife," Peg clucked.

Gene quickly reached into the back pocket of his Levi's and pulled out his utility knife. "Don't worry, I got old Betsy right here," he said grinning triumphantly.

Bev and Dan laughed as Peg rolled her eyes.

"Where do you keep your tools, Sonny?" Gene asked.

"In the woodshed, Dad."

"Where are your Christmas decorations, Dan?" his mother asked. "We'll start on your house next."

Bev quickly looked from Peg to Dan. Her eyes widened. She knew Dan had never decorated for Christmas or even put up a tree since he moved here, and she knew why. There was total silence as Peg waited for an answer.

"I … I … don't—" Dan's voice faltered.

The sudden sound of Jimmy Buffett singing "Bama Breeze" and a vibration in Dan's front pocket broke the tension. Dan reached for his phone.

His voice cracked as he answered. "Hello?"

A crying woman's voice came from the other end. "Dan, something terrible has happened."

Dan instantly recognized the voice. "April, what's the matter?" Every hair on Dan's body stood on end. He looked to his empty glass' wishing it were full again.

Dan's mind quickly flashed back to another, similar call.

"Mr. Coast, this is Trooper Stevens, with the New York State Police. Mr. Coast, there's been an accident."

"An accident? What are you talking about?"

"It's your wife, Mr. Coast. She was in an automobile accident this afternoon. Can you come down to the hospital, Mr. Coast?"

"Is she okay?"

"I think it's better if you just come down to the hospital and speak with the doctors, Mr. Coast."

April's quavering voice brought Dan back to the present day. "Dan … it's … it's Phil. He … he was shot this morning."

Chapter Six

"I'm sorry, sir, like I've already told you, if you're not an immediate family member I can't let you into Mr. Lambert's room." A very large nurse holding a clip board stood in front of Phil Lambert's door. She was probably sixty years old but her hair was pulled back so tightly that any wrinkles she may have had were now replaced by a permanent look of surprise. She was wearing extra-large blue scrubs stretched over a double extra-large body. The yellow "Have a nice day" smiley faces decorating her scrub top did not convey her current mood.

"He's my husband," Dan replied straight-faced.

"But Mr. Lambert has a *wife*."

"He's a Mormon."

"A Mormon?"

"Yeah, a big ole' gay Mormon."

"Can I help you with something, sir?" came a voice from behind Dan.

Dan turned to see a police officer walking down the hall toward him. The officer was carrying a paper cup filled with coffee in one hand and a large jelly donut in the other. The bite that had been taken out of the jelly bun had left a small glob of jelly on the officer's shirt as well as traces of powdered sugar in the corners of his mouth. The officer came to a stop a few feet in front of Dan. "Oh, it's *you*," he said nastily.

Dan shot back, "Top o' the morning to you, too, Parker.

"You know this man, officer?" the nurse asked.

"Yeah, I know him. He's a local beach bum. Thinks he's a private detective," the officer replied, his eyes never leaving Dan's.

"Nurse Ratched here won't let me in to see Phil," Dan said, nodding his head toward the disgruntled nurse.

"Why would she?" the cop answered. "I'll take it from here, nurse."

"He'll take it from here, nurse," Dan repeated.

The nurse took one last look at Dan and spun on her heels like a military cadet and returned to her station behind a reception desk. Within seconds her mouth was filled with Double Stuf Oreos from a half-eaten package on the desk.

"Listen Coast, your buddy is in a lot of trouble if he makes it through this," said Parker "We found three kilos of coke on the floor of his truck."

"Are you sure it wasn't Diet Coke? He's been trying to drop a few pounds ever since someone mistook him for a cop." Dan's eyes went from the jelly bun to the unsightly stain on the cop's uniform.

Parker moved in closer. "Listen, smartass," he said through clenched teeth. "That mouth of yours is going to get you in a lot of trouble someday."

Dan moved in closer. "And that purty mouth of yours

has powdered sugar all over it."

Forgetting his hands were full and spilling his coffee and smashing his jelly bun, Parker grabbed Dan by the front of his shirt just as two arms shot between them, separating the two men.

"Break it up, break it up!" yelled Rick Carver, Key West's portly police chief, in his thick Southern drawl.

Both men backed away. The officer walked to the desk and grabbed some tissue to wipe the jelly from his fingers.

"Look what he did to my shirt!" Dan complained, picking bits of donut and jelly from his shirt.

Rick looked to the officer. "Parker, go to the restroom and clean yourself up, for Chrissakes." Then he turned to Dan. "Always causing trouble, aren't ya?"

"*He* started it," Dan said, pointing down the hall.

"*You* started it," Parker shot back as he rounded the corner and disappeared into the restroom.

"Come on," said Rick, motioning toward Phil's door. He went in and Dan followed.

Dan stood at Phil Lambert's bedside. His eyes went from the two IV bags that hung from a stainless steel pole on wheels to the wires that connected to the patches stuck to Phil's chest. The sight of the tracheal tube protruding grotesquely from Phil's mouth prompted a surge of bile to rise in Dan's throat. The only sound was beeping and the sound of air being pumped into Phil's lungs. "Jesus Christ," was the only thing Dan could say. He stepped closer and put his hand on Phil's arm.

Rick took off his gold-framed aviator sunglasses with orange-tinted lenses and folded them into the front of his shirt. He leaned his back against the wall, his arms folded and resting on his large belly, which strained the buttons on his dark navy short-sleeved shirt to the point of popping. Dan noticed the large pit stains and the dried residue of a leaky ink pen in both pleated pockets, which bulged with wrinkled documents, chewed-on pencils and pens, a tire gauge, and a dandruff-flecked comb. The chief's black leather shoes were scuffed and cruddy and hadn't seen a shoeshine rag in years. *Just look at that slob,* Dan thought, *and yet he thinks the sun rises and sets on his ass!*

Rick cleared his throat noisily and drawled, "He's gonna be booked on possession with intent to sell when he comes around."

"Come on, Rick, you know Phil wasn't into anything like that. There's gotta be some kind of mistake. I know Phil woul—"

"Dan, I know he's your friend," Rick cut in. "but how well do you really know anybody? He's got a plane, boats, jet-skis. His business is the perfect cover for this kind of thing. Think about it, where does he get all the money for those toys? Maybe he got into some financial trouble. Maybe he saw this as his only way out."

"There's no way, Rick."

Rick waved his big oven mitt of a hand dismissively. "I'm waiting on a search warrant for his business, home, and bank records. I should get the call any minute. We'll get to the bottom—"

The door opened and April Lambert walked in. She burst into tears, went to Dan and threw her arms around him.

"It'll be all right, April." Dan patted her back. "We'll find out who did this."

"I'll find out who did this," Rick said. "You're gonna stay the hell out of it and let us do our jobs."

Dan bit his tongue. He marveled that this overfed Barney Fife managed to keep his cushy job despite a raft of botched investigations in recent years. To say there was no love lost between them was the understatement of the century, but they had formed and maintained a begrudging tolerance for each other.

A phone rang and Rick reached for his shirt pocket. "Hello … okay … alright. Okay, I'll be there in fifteen minutes." Rick hung up his cell phone. "We got our warrant. I'm gonna head over to Island Adventures first, April. Do you want to be there while we are?"

April released her grip on Dan. "No … just go." She waved her hand and sat down in a chair next to Phil's bed. "Just go."

"I'll go instead," Dan offered.

"The hell you will," Rick responded. "You go anywhere near that place before we're done and you'll find yourself in a cell downtown." Rick slowly and with great care put his sunglasses back on, just the way he had probably practiced in front of a mirror a thousand times and walked out the door.

Dan shook his head. "I'd like to shove those sunglasses up his ass someday."

Chapter Seven

Dan turned right off of Thirteenth on to Flagler. He could feel the warm salt air blow through the hair on his left arm as it hung over the side of the door. The sun was warm on his face. His sunglasses were barely doing their job. By now his hangover was in full swing. His head was pounding, and he was sure he had only rented his breakfast. The stereo was tuned to Radio Margaritaville and Jim White was singing a song about some research he had been conducting.

Grabbing the steering wheel with his left hand, Dan fiddled for the cell phone in the pocket of his blue cargo shorts. When he had retrieved it he dialed Red's number.

An annoyed response came from the other end. "Yeah?"

"What's your problem?" Dan returned.

"Dishwashers."

"Broken?" Dan asked.

"Not the dishwasher, the kid who does the dishes … and yeah, I think he's broken. Something in his head is broken. Ya know, I hired that kid 'cause his mother—"

Dan cut him off. "Spare me the soap opera details of your morning. I just wanted to make sure you were at the bar. I'm on my way over there now."

Red detected a certain tone in Dan's voice. "Is something wrong?"

"I'll explain when I get there." Dan ended the call and tossed his cell into the passenger seat. It bounced and fell between the door and the seat. Dan rolled his eyes and shook his head. Supertramp began singing Long Way Home. He rolled his eyes again and shut off the radio.

*****

Dan pulled the Porsche off of Charles Lake Road and into Red's gravel parking lot. He skidded to a stop and then backed into a spot across from the front door.

Lunch had begun at eleven but there were no customers yet. Dan made his way to the bar and climbed aboard one of the many orange barstools that lined the bar. The bar floor was wet and the room smelled of pine. Dan rested his forearms on the edge of the bar. It felt cool and clean. He put his forehead against the bar and let out his breath as though he had been holding it all day.

"Last night finally catching up with you, pal?" Red asked as he exited the kitchen, letting the large wooden door swing shut behind him.

"What time did I leave here last night?" Dan asked, never removing his head from the bar.

"You were gone by midnight. You and that girl with

the purple hair."

"Purple hair?"

"The one you were singing karaoke with."

Dan slowly raised his head from the bar. "I sang karaoke?"

"Not real well. She was good though, and what a body."

"I left *with* her?"

"Sure did, pal. How did that turn out?"

"I have no idea. I woke up about a block from my house around nine o'clock. Some little midget was standing over me trying to wake me."

"Little person."

"Yeah, he was little. I think the word midget covered that," Dan said rubbing his temples.

"No, I mean they don't like to be called midgets. They like to be called little people."

"Since when?"

"It's like you live in a rock." Red changed the subject. "What did you come over here to tell me anyway?"

"Oh yeah, the guy that got shot this morning." Dan said.

"Yeah, what about him?" Red's eyes went from the glass he was polishing to Dan.

"It was Phil."

"Our Phil?"

"Yeah, our Phil."

"Jesus Christ, Dan, you don't think you should have led with that story?"

"Sorry. You got me sidetracked."

"Is he going to be okay?"

"They're not sure yet. He's in a coma. April said the doctors told her that if he makes it through the next couple of days his chance of survival is a lot greater."

"What the hell happened?"

Dan put his hands out in front of him; palms down and side by side, he moved them up and down imitating a pair of scales. "Make me a drink first. I have to get back to level." He dropped his hands to the bar.

Red poured Dan's usual tequila, Seven, and lime and slid it to him across the bar. Dan took a big swig and put the glass back on the bar. It was less than half full. Red knew that Dan needed that drink way more than he wanted it. He also knew that it was the same story every Christmas. Red had seen it all before. Sometime around Thanksgiving it would start. Dan's drinking would increase. He would start getting pretty moody, stop shaving. The drinking would increase a little more, and then a week or so before Christmas, Dan would be drunk most of the day. Come Christmas Eve, Dan would disappear and no one would see him until a day or so after the New Year. Red would stop by, so would Bev and Phil, but Dan wouldn't answer the door. *What would this year bring, now that Dan's parents were here?* Red wondered.

Dan began telling the story of Phil's shooting and the suspected drug dealing. By the end of the story Dan had finished his second drink and asked for another. Red pretended not to hear him and looked behind him at the clock.

"You gonna make me another one? Christ, it's like being in rehab," Dan grumbled.

Red wanted to say that maybe rehab might be a good idea, but bit his tongue and tried a different approach.

"Maybe you should try and keep a clear head, Dan. After all, someone has to find out what really happened to Phil."

Dan fell for it. "Yeah you're probably right." He got up from the stool. His flip-flop snagged on the leg of the stool and he stumbled against the bar. "Maybe two *was* enough," he joked.

Red smiled and picked up Dan's glass and dumped the ice into the sink. "What's our first move?"

Dan thought for a second and then said, "First I want to take a look at Phil's truck. Then I want to head over to where the shooting took place and have a look around."

"Sounds good," Red replied. "Why don't you head on home and get some rest, visit with your parents for a while. I'll run by your place and pick you up around six and we'll go from there."

Dan nodded and went toward the door. When he reached the door he stopped but didn't turn around. "It's live *under* a rock, not live *in* a rock."

"Ya couldn't let it go, ya bastard."

Dan grinned and walked through the door.

Chapter Eight

Dan decided to take a little detour around to the liquor store on Bertha Street to stock up. After all, he told himself, it *was* the holiday season and his parents *were* in town.

Dan grabbed a small plastic basket as he entered the store. The woman behind the counter looked up from her magazine and smiled. She had a pretty smile that caused Dan to stare just a second too long. He quickly noticed her dimples and a few freckles that dotted her cheeks. Her hair was dark and curly. Dan smiled back and made his way toward the tequila section.

He grabbed a bottle of Jose Quervo and a bottle of Dos Manos. Dan slowly moved down the aisle and picked up a bottle each of rum and whiskey. He placed them in the basket and went to the checkout counter.

"New here?" Dan asked. "Haven't seen you before today."

The freckled salesclerk smiled again, setting off those beautiful dimples. "Yeah, started this shift a couple of weeks ago. I work part time over at the Waffle House too."

"Busy beaver, huh?"

"Something like that. All set?"

Dan placed his finger about three quarters of the way down the bottle of tequila. "I'm not all set till its right about here."

The woman laughed, revealing very small lines around her eyes. Dan guessed her age at about thirty-nine or forty. "Good one," she said. "Name's Jeanie."

"Make it Dan."

Dan paid with cash, as usual, and Jeanie grabbed two paper bags from under the counter. She placed two bottles of booze into each bag, wedged a small piece of cardboard between each bottle, and slid them across the counter to him and said, "Thanks, you have a good one."

"That's what I've been told," Dan grinned.

Jeanie shook her head with an embarrassed grin and returned to her magazine. *Wow!* Dan thought as he walked through the door. *Freckles, dimples, and a damned good sense of humor.* He had always been a sucker for all three. He mentally put her on his "to do" list.

"To do" list. That's crude, Coast, even for you. He had made a half-assed effort to abandon his womanizing ways but old habits die hard.

Old habits die hard. The chinking of the bottles he carried sure as hell proved that.

*****

As Dan rounded the corner onto George Street he

noticed a group of boys gathered at the corner of Sky View Street. They stood in the street, and Dan slowed to drive around them. *Goddamn kids, why do they have to stand in the road? What's wrong with the sidewalk?* He started to beep the horn but refrained, realizing he was acting like a crotchety old man.

As he slowly passed the group he noticed they were all boys, around twelve or thirteen years old. They stood in a circle, and in the middle was a smaller boy that Dan recognized as the young man who had awakened him that morning. *Noah, yeah, that was the kid's name.*

Noah turned and looked into Dan's eyes just as one of the boys shoved him to the ground and yelled, "Stupid midget freak!" Dan clenched his jaw.

He pulled his car to the curb a few yards away from the group, climbed out, and started walking toward the boys. He knew he couldn't smack any of the kids, but he also knew someone should. As he reached the circle of rowdies they separated and Dan reached out his hand to Noah. Noah took it and Dan pulled him to his feet.

"Go get in my car," Dan said.

"But my mother told me to never get—"

"In my car. Now."

Noah did as he was told and headed toward Dan's car, looking back once as he pulled the door handle. Nothing happened.

"The door's broken," Dan yelled. "You have to climb over."

Dan and the group of boys watched for what seemed like an eternity as Noah struggled to climb over the door. He finally gave up and walked around and got in on the driver's side.

Dan returned his focus to the group of boys and curtly

nodded his head. "Take off."

The boys quickly began to disburse. Dan put his hand on the boy's shoulder that had pushed Noah. "Not you," he said.

Dan waited till the other kids were out of earshot and turned back to the young man. "What's your name?" he demanded.

"Gale," the boy answered.

"Gale? That's a girl's name."

The boy said nothing.

"You have a girl's name and you're picking on that kid?" Dan said, pointing toward Noah.

"It was my grandfather's name," the boy protested lamely. His throat was dry and his voice shook.

"Did your grandfather pick on people too?"

"I don't think so."

Dan looked around the street one more time. Two of the boys remained a few yards away. Dan looked back at Gale. "Listen, Girly Gale," he said, loud enough for the other boys to hear. Then he leaned over closer and whispered, "If you ever pick on Noah again or call him a freak I'm going to rip off your Goddamn arms and let him beat you to death with them. Got it?"

Gale's eyes widened and he shook his head yes.

Dan lowered his eyebrows and glared at the boy. "Do you believe me?"

Gale once again shook his head yes.

"Good," Dan said and walked back toward his car. Behind him he heard one of the boys giggle and say, "Girly Gale. Ha, ha!"

Coasts of Christmas Past

Gale yelled, "Shut up!"

Dan grinned big as he climbed in his car.

Chapter Nine

Dan pulled his car to the curb in front of Noah's house. He left the engine running as he climbed out, letting Noah climb over the driver's seat and exit the car.

"What the hell was that all about?" Dan asked.

Noah shrugged, "Nothing."

"It didn't look like nothing."

"They were just picking on me."

"I could see that. Why were they picking on you?"

"Because I'm a little person."

Dan let out a sigh as he raked his fingers through this hair. He looked around the neighborhood as though he was searching for something to say. He crouched down so he was eye to eye with Noah. "You know they're just assholes, right?"

Noah grinned. There was a small tear in the corner of his eye.

"People like those guys are just unhappy and they don't like themselves very much. They think the only way for them to be happy is to make someone else unhappier than them." Dan stared into the boy's eyes. "You understand?"

Noah nodded his head yes, and wiped his eye with the back of his hand. He turned and started up the cement pathway to his front door.

Dan looked to the empty driveway. "Your mother or father home?" he called out.

Noah stopped and turned halfway. "My mom works till eight."

"Your dad?"

"He's not here either."

"How old are ya, kid?" Dan asked.

"Nine."

"Do you stay by yourself a lot at night?"

"Just two nights a week. My mom works right over there," Noah pointed in the direction they had come, "at the liquor store."

"On Bertha?"

"Yeah."

So freckles was married, eh? Dan was disgusted with his earlier impure thoughts. He had scruples, after all. Not many, but he had them. "Alright, get on in the house."

Noah turned and Dan watched as he finished his trek up the walkway and to his front door. Noah reached into his front pocket and pulled out a key, inserted it into the doorknob and gave it a turn. He pushed the door open, turned back to Dan and gave a small wave. Dan returned the gesture.

"Make sure you lock the door behind you," Dan called out. He stood at the edge of the street until Noah closed the door and, in the quiet of the evening, Dan heard the lock click.

Dan climbed back into his car and turned the key. The grinding of the starter against the fly wheel quickly reminded Dan that the engine was already running. *Goddammit!*

Chapter Ten

Dan pulled his beat-up old Porsche into the driveway of his modest beach bungalow at 632 Beach View Street. He turned off the engine and looked at the bottles of booze tucked away in their paper bags in the seat beside him. *Dan, drink us,* he could have sworn he heard one of them say. He reached his hand into one of the bags and pulled out the bottle of Dos Manos. He looked around for witnesses. He saw none. He breathed in slowly through his nose. There was a faint aroma of a gas flame burning the remnants of past steaks and sea food off in the distance.

Dan unscrewed the bottle and took a big, long drink. By the time the bottle left his lips almost a quarter of its contents were gone. Dan let out a sigh and put his head back on the headrest. He remembered when a drink like that would have burned his throat and taken his breath away. He sat looking up into the sky, watching the clouds slowly drift by. A seagull flew over, and then another. *If I get shit on …* Dan thought. He screwed the cap back on tightly and slid it under his seat.

As Dan exited his car he could hear voices coming from his backyard. He walked down the gravel pathway that led from the driveway to his back yard. His father sat in one Adirondack chair next to the fire pit and his mother relaxed in the other one. She was more than halfway through a bottle of Diet Pepsi.

Gene sat still with the crossword puzzle from this morning's newspaper folded neatly in his lap. His head was tilted down and his sagging face appeared as though it was slowly melting off the front of his skull. He was sound asleep. His pen lay on the ground beside his chair where it had slipped from his fingers as he nodded off.

"I was wondering when you would get home," Peg said as she looked up and saw Dan getting closer.

"I had a few errands to run," Dan answered.

"At the liquor store?" Peg nodded toward the two bags in Dan's arm.

Dan grinned. "One man's errand…"

"Your father ran to the store and grabbed some steaks and salt potatoes while you were gone. Bev just lit her grill. We're going to eat over at her place."

"Sounds good."

Gene stopped breathing for a few seconds and then let out a noise that sounded like part snore, part choking, and part death rattle. He opened his eyes and looked at Peg and then to Dan with a look of disgust and irritation. A look that told them that they were somehow to blame for his awakening.

"What are you looking at?" Gene grunted.

"You. Ya stopped breathing. We thought you had finally kicked the bucket." Dan answered grinning.

"Funny," Gene replied.

"Seems like he goes fifteen or twenty minutes at a time during the night without breathing," Peg put in.

Dan raised his eyebrows. "Fifteen or twenty

minutes?"

"That's what it seems like. I spend half the night awake wondering if he's dead yet."

"What do ya mean, 'yet'? Gene asked. "'Yet', means you're just lying there wishing I was dead."

"Not wishing, just waiting," Peg said with a smirk.

Dan laughed out loud, turned and headed toward the back door. Gene noticed the bags in his hand. "Oh good," he said. "Ya stopped at the liquor store. Make us a couple of drinks. I felt like I was in rehab sitting here."

Dan smiled. He liked his father's sense of humor, and so did most everyone else. Many of Dan's one-liners came from his father. "Rehab," he whispered to himself. "Good one, Dad."

Dan returned a few moments later with two drinks in his hand and the bottle of Quervo under his arm. His mother had left her seat and was walking up Bev's steps to her back deck.

He handed his father his drink and then sat in the other chair. He placed the bottle of booze in the dirt next to the chair.

Dan was starting to feel the effects of the big drink of tequila he had downed in the car earlier. He felt as though his speech was slurring. He tried to hide it, but he knew that's when others usually noticed it even more.

"Have a few at Red's?" his father questioned.

Shit, he noticed. Dan knew that when he started feeling guilty about his drinking that that meant he was drinking way too much. "Yeah. I had one," he said.

"Just one?"

"Dad, please. You sound like Mom," Dan quickly responded.

Gene put up his hands in surrender. "Okay, okay, just asking. Just making sure you're okay. Your mother and I worry about you down here by yourself. You should come home for the holidays."

"Why, so everyone can look at me with that same look you have on your face right now?"

"What look?"

"That, *oh, poor guy, he can't get over his wife's death, so he has to spend the holidays alone* look," Dan replied in a childish, almost taunting tone.

Gene took a sip of his drink and said nothing. He could see the pain in his son's eyes and it broke his heart. This was usually a good time for a smartass remark or a stupid one-liner for lightening things up, but Gene could think of nothing to say.

There was a long silence and then Dan said, "You're right, Dad, I can't get over it. I think about her a hundred times a day. I dream about her almost every night." He paused to catch his breath. "I thought moving down here would be better. I thought that there wouldn't be so many things to remind me of her, but at the same time I thought living here would make me feel closer to her in some way. This time of the year is worse. Christmas was always a spec—" Dan could feel his throat drying and constricting as he spoke. He stopped and rubbed his eyes and took a big swig of his drink.

Gene still sat quietly. He wished there was something he could do to take away his son's pain. He downed his drink.

"Boys," came Bev's voice from her back deck. "Come and get it!"

Dan and his father both rose at the same time, same speed and with the same groan. As Dan passed by his father, Gene put his hand on his son's shoulder. Gene didn't know what to say but the firm hand on his shoulder told Dan exactly what Gene wanted to say.

"Thanks Dad," Dan whispered.

As the two men walked side by side toward Bev's house, Red's voice boomed from behind them. "Something sure smells good."

Gene whispered to his son, "Never misses a free meal, does he?"

Chapter Eleven

Bev, Gene, and Peg sat on one side of the picnic table and Dan and Red on the other. An empty plate sat in front of each person as well as half empty glasses. Silverware and used napkins were strewn about the table. It was obvious a feeding frenzy had taken place only moments earlier. The thin plastic red and white checkered tablecloth billowed slightly in the evening breeze.

"Can I get anyone anything else?" Bev asked the group. "Another drink maybe."

Dan lifted his glass. "I'll have another drin—"

"No we're good," Red jumped in.

Dan shot Red a look. "We're?" he asked.

"I just meant maybe we should... I mean, you said you wanted to go over and take a look at Phil's truck. Maybe go over to the scene and take a look around."

Dan stood and grabbed the half empty bottle of tequila off the table. "If I want another goddamn drink, I'll have another goddamn drink." He turned and teetered toward the steps. "What are you my mother?"

"No, but I am," Peg put in, "and I think maybe you've had enough."

"I'm a grown man. I think I know when I've had enough."

Dan walked super-carefully down the steps, across the yard, and toward the beach. The dinner party watched as he staggered to the sand, turned, and disappeared out of sight.

"Should one of us follow him?" said Peg worriedly. "I'm afraid he might do something foolish. He might drown!"

"I'm with Peg," Bev agreed "He's in a bad way."

Gene pushed himself up from the bench. "Guess I'm elected. You gals worry too much." He followed Dan's trail, and it was evident to all from the look on his face that he shared that worry, but his masculine pride wouldn't let him say so.

"Well, I think I've had enough for one evening," Red said as he put his large hands on the table and pushed himself to his feet.

Peg reached out and put her hand on Red's. "Red, thanks for calling us. You're right, he does seem to be getting worse."

Chapter Twelve

Dan loved everything about bacon. He loved eating it, he loved cooking it, he loved smelling it, and he loved the sound of its sizzle as it lay frying in the pan. He reached for the tongs that stood among the other utensils in the stainless steel container on the countertop next to the stove. One by one he picked up the strips and turned them over. He took a deep breath through his nose and let out a luxurious "ahh." *God, that smells good*, he thought.

Dan jerked slightly as a small bit of grease popped off of the pan and landed on his bare chest. *Ouch!*

"Alex!" he yelled up toward the gravity-fed vent in the kitchen ceiling that led to their bedroom. There was no answer. "Alex!" he yelled again, a little louder this time.

"What?" he heard her respond from the vent.

"Can you bring my T-shirt off the floor when you come down?"

"Ye-*esss*," she sang out, turning her response into two syllables.

"Thank you," he sang back sarcastically.

Dan leaned over to assess the flame and then turned the dial to low. He turned the bacon once again.

Alex entered the kitchen. Her long brown hair was pulled back into a tight ponytail. She wore a black wife beater and white shorts. Dan stared at her as she approached him. *God, you're beautiful*, he thought.

She handed him his T-shirt and leaned in for a kiss. She placed the palm of her hand on his chest. Their lips touched and made a faint smack. She looked up into his eyes and smiled.

"Do you still love me?" she whispered.

*****

"Yes," he said loudly as he awoke, startled.

Dan was lying on his side. He slowly pushed himself up on his elbows and looked around the room. He could still smell the bacon. He took his thumb and middle finger and ground them into his eyes as if this would magically make him aware of his surroundings. He looked around the room again. He was in his own bed.

Dan sat up and scooted to the bottom of the bed and put his feet on something warm and furry. It was Buddy.

"Decided to stop by?" he asked the dog. He reached down and scratched the dog between the ears. "Come on, shithead; let's see what's for breakfast."

Dan was still dressed in yesterday's shorts. His right arm was still in its sleeve, as though he had attempted to get undressed. He slid the other arm into its sleeve and, leaving the shirt unbuttoned, he went to the kitchen. Buddy didn't follow.

Peg was removing strips of bacon from a pan and laying them flat on a paper towel she had folded on the countertop. Without turning around she said, "Good morning sleepy head."

"Morning Mom," Dan replied, scratching his head.

"Scrambled or over medium?"

Dan felt his stomach turn. "Better make it scrambled."

"Scrambled it is."

Peg cracked three eggs into a bowl and began beating them to death with a fork. Dan poured himself a cup of coffee and took a sip.

"I thought you said you were going to remodel this kitchen the last time we were here."

Dan rolled his eyes but didn't respond. He sipped his coffee.

"Didn't you say that?" Peg poured the eggs into a pan.

"Yes. I … think I might have mentioned it."

"How come you haven't even started it?"

Dan's voice went up three octaves. "I don't know."

"Well, you always say you're going to do something but you never do."

Dan raised his voice. "I guess I'm just a goddamn liar," he said as he shoved open the screen door and walked down the steps.

Gene sat in one of the Adirondack chairs reading this morning's edition of the Key West Citizen. His coffee sat on the ground next to him. Dan took a seat in the other chair.

Gene leaned over and picked up his coffee cup and took a sip. "Ya know, you could use a little table next to each one of these chairs," he said.

Dan shot him a look. "Why, did I say I was going to buy a couple of goddamn tables?"

Gene looked confused.

"Sorry, Dad," Dan said with the wave of a hand.

"Rough night, Sonny?" Gene asked.

"Who knows," was Dan's reply.

Gene took a section of the paper he had already read, leaned forward, and handed it to Dan. Dan took the paper and laid it on his lap.

"Ya got in kinda late," Gene said.

"Oh yeah?" Dan took a drink of coffee and looked out in the direction of the beach. A runner ran by and then another. A sea gull laughed.

"Three-thirty."

Dan kept his eyes on the horizon. *Three-thirty*, he thought, *what the hell did I do until three-thirty?*

The back door creaked and both men looked up to see Peg's arm pushing it open to let the dog out. Buddy made his way down the gravel path that led to the fire pit and lay down between the two chairs. Gene went back to reading his paper. Dan looked back toward the beach.

"Any plans for the day?" Dan asked his father.

"We were thinking about heading out to that Fort Zachary Taylor. Your mom wanted to see it the last time we were here but we didn't have enough time. How about you?"

"I gotta get my head straight, Dad. I gotta lay off the booze a little. I told April I would find out what happened to Phil but when I start drinking, I just don't know when to stop. I don't know what's wrong with me … I mean, I know what's wrong with me, but Christ, *what's wrong with me?* Ya know what I mean?"

Gene shook his head. It wasn't a yes, or a no, just a shake. "Maybe you should talk to someone," he said.

"I *am* talking to someone. *You.*"

The back door opened again. "Breakfast is ready."

Buddy jumped up and headed for the door.

Chapter Thirteen

Dan Coast pulled into the parking lot of Red's Bar and Grill around eleven-thirty. He skidded to a stop on the crushed stone, threw it into reverse, and backed into a parking spot. Dan sat for a moment staring at Red's front door. He looked around the parking lot, and there were three other cars. Reaching under his seat Dan pulled out the bottle of tequila he had placed there the day before. He unscrewed the cap, took a drink, replaced the cap and slid the bottle back into its hiding place.

As Dan walked across the parking lot toward the door he wondered where he was all night, how he got home, and why his left hip and knee were hurting. He wondered if he had fallen in his drunken stupor. He wondered if anyone had seen him fall and didn't want to help a stumbling foolish old drunk. Or maybe someone did help him and he just didn't remember.

"What's up, a-hole," came Red's voice from behind the bar as he polished a glass and hung it in the rack above his head.

"Not much, douche bag," Dan responded.

Red pulled the glass he had just placed in the rack

back out and slammed it in the ice tray under the bar, filling it with ice, and placed it on the bar. He reached into the well and pulled out a bottle of cheap tequila.

Dan put his hand over the glass. "No, I'm good. Just 7-UP."

Red didn't argue. He put the bottle back in its resting place, grabbed the soda gun, and filled the glass. "Lime?"

"Sure, at least it will look like a drink."

Red opened the fruit tray lid and stabbed a lime wedge with a tiny green sword and tossed it into the glass.

Dan took a sip just as if it were tequila. His tongue, brain, and body weren't fooled.

"Hey, sorry about last night," Dan said, staring at his faux drink.

Red ignored the statement. "So what's first?"

"We'll play it by ear," Dan replied. He downed his drink and dismounted the stool.

Red walked over to the wooden, swinging kitchen door and pushed it open a crack. "Jocko," he yelled.

Jock let out a grunt in the form of a question.

"You have the con," Red hollered.

Jock let out another grunt.

"That new girl will be here at noon," Red added. "Make sure she leaves her goddamn cell phone in her car."

Another grunt.

Dan and Red headed for the door.

Shaking his head Red said, "I sure hope Cindy gets her ass back here from Chicago soon. I've gone through three bartenders in three months."

"Yeah," Dan replied. "I'm wondering what April is

going to do without Derrick here now that Phil is in the hospital."

As the two men reached the Porsche, Dan pulled his phone from his pocket, tapped the screen a few times, and placed it to his ear. "April. It's Dan. How's Phil doing? … Good …Yeah …yup … we'll be there in a few minutes." Dan placed the phone back in his pocket.

"How's he doin'?" Red asked.

"No worse, no better."

Dan started the Porsche and gunned it. The car fishtailed, kicking stones in every direction.

Red picked himself up off the floorboard. "Have ya gotta do that *every* time you leave here?"

Chapter Fourteen

"So, where's his truck?" Dan asked.

April Lambert sat in the office of Island Adventures behind a large desk, her elbows on the desk and her forehead resting on the palms of her hands. "Still at police impound," she said wearily.

Dan let out a loud sigh.

"Gonna be kind of tough to have a look at it, then," Red snorted.

Dan shot him a withering *shut the fuck up, you're not helping* look and scanned the office. The file cabinet drawers were open and the files were gone. The computer that sat on Phil's desk was missing, as were the printer and phone.

Red walked to a table that sat next to the file cabinets and picked up a broken coffee pot. "Real careful, weren't they?" he said, shaking his head.

Dan used his toe to move around some papers that lay on the floor. "I don't think we'll find any clues here."

"Where exactly did the shooting take place?" Red

asked, straightening a picture that was hanging on the wall above the table.

April looked up slowly. Her eyes were baggy and red-rimmed. "Chief Carver said it happened near the corner of Riviera and Eleventh."

"We'll start there I guess," Dan said. "Did Carver say what time it happened?"

April had to think. "Let's see … around six-thirty."

"Where was he going?" Red asked.

Dan lowered his brow and gave Red the old *I'll ask the questions here* look. Red raised his hands in surrender. "Sorry, Columbo," he joked.

"Where *was* he going, April?" Dan repeated.

"He went out to get donuts for the customers like he does every morning around five-thirty. I usually leave our house around six and meet him over here. I called his cell about six-forty-five but it went right to voice mail. Then I got the call from Chief Carver around seven-thirty."

Red looked back to the table where the donuts were supposed to be and let out a longing "*Hmmmm.*"

It was April's turn to give Red the stink eye. Dan knew they would be stopping for donuts now.

"Uh, April, where did he usually get donuts?" Red asked sheepishly like the insensitive bastard he was.

"Glazed Donuts, Over on—"

"Eaton Street," Red finished, nodding his head. He was fairly drooling.

April lowered her head and began sobbing. "He loved their Key lime pie donuts."

"Oh my God, I love tho—" Red stopped abruptly when he saw Dan's expression.

Dan clenched his jaw and a serious look came over his face. "April," he said. "Has anything out of the ordinary been going on around here in the last few days, anything with Phil? Has he been acting different? Has he had a run-in with any customers? Has his mood changed? Has he been quieter? Can you think of anything at all? Think hard, the smallest detail might help."

April stared back at Dan and slowly shook her head no. "Nothing," she responded. "But I know that it has nothing to do with drugs, that's for sure. I don't care what they think they found in his truck."

"I know, April. We'll get to the bottom of this," Dan said.

Red turned and pushed the office door open and walked out first. Dan caught it with his foot as it began to shut and walked out behind him. A bell over the door rang as it shut and Dan turned to see the SORRY WE'RE CLOSED sign swinging against the glass. He grimaced and shook his head.

As the two men reached Dan's car Red paused and glanced out over Phil's dock at his boat bobbing in the incoming tide. "You know what I could really go for?"

"A donut."

Red quickly looked to Dan. "You read my mind."

"It's a quick read, pal."

Chapter Fifteen

Dan took a right off Flagler onto Eleventh Street just as Red was cramming his third donut into his mouth. He chased it down with a big gulp of chocolate milk.

Dan said, "Now the woman at the donut shop said th—"

"Carla," Red interrupted over a mouthful of strawberry filled goodness.

"Yeah... Carla said that she remembered Phil pulling up in front just as she unlocked the door at a few minutes after six," Dan said. He pulled to the side of the street behind an empty boat trailer. A vacant lot overgrown with small trees and shrubs was to their right and Riviera ran perpendicular to their left. Eleventh Street was a dead end with a small boat launch into a canal.

"April said he left the house at six," Red added.

"So he went straight from their house to the bakery."

"But why did he do a complete three-sixty after he left the donut shop and end up over on Riviera?" Red mused. "Island Adventures is in the opposite direction."

Dan debated whether or not to correct him. Red was his best friend, but he was also the undisputed king of the malapropism, the great Norm Crosby had *nothing* on Red. It annoyed the hell out of Dan, and nine times out of ten he just couldn't let Red's mangling of words and idioms slide, even though this always led to even more consternation.

"One-eighty," Dan said after a brief silence.

"One-eighty what?"

"He did a one-eighty, not a three-sixty."

"No, he turned all the way around and went in the opposite direction," Red said, pointing his finger in the air and twirling it in a circle.

"If he turned all the way around he would have been going back in the same direction!" Dan's voice grew louder and his grip on the steering wheel tightened.

Red's reply was low and slow, calm and measured. "*Noooo*, he went in the wrong direction."

"I know, but if he we—" Dan stopped quickly and got out of the car. "Forget it." *Jesus Christ, how do I get myself into a conversation like that?* He thought about reaching under the seat for something to calm him down but refrained.

"Ya get it now?" Red asked as he climbed over the passenger side door.

"Yeah," Dan said rubbing the back of his neck with his thumb and fingers.

Together they crossed Eleventh Street toward the corner of Riviera. Dan walked over to a three and a half foot concrete fence that bordered the yard of the first house they came to. He looked over the fence at the ground and then at the ground on their side of the fence.

"What are you looking for?" Red asked.

"I don't know," Dan answered.

"That's what I figured."

Dan pointed at a fresh black tire track on the sidewalk that ended just short of a fire hydrant. "Looks like this is where he stopped," he said.

Red searched the road nearby. "There's no blood anywhere on the road."

"And April said he had lost a *lot* of blood," Dan added.

"Maybe they shot him in the truck."

"Or maybe he was shot somewhere else and moved here."

Red had a surprised look on his face and grinned.

"What?" Dan asked.

"Look who's turning into a real PI," Red answered.

"I saw it on an old episode of *Jake and the Fat Man* last week."

"Oh shit, I loved that show! Hey, remember that *Hardcastle and McCormick*?"

Dan grinned with sweet memory. "Aw, I loved that car!"

"Yeah, the Coyote, you should get a car like—"

"Can I help you gentlemen?" came a voice from behind the concrete wall.

Dan and Red turned to see a grotesquely large man in tan Bermuda shorts, and no shirt covering his hairy chest, approaching them. He wore brown leather sandals with white socks stretched tightly to a point just below his knees. The man's shorts were stretched over his mammoth belly and pulled up so high that he almost could have used them as a bra for his jouncing double D man boobs. Just as disgusting, he had one of those *way*-outie bellybuttons that looked like a miniature doorknob.

"Where's Jake?" Red quipped out of the corner of his mouth.

Dan tried to hide his grin. "Good day, sir. We're investigating the shooting."

"You are, are ya?" he said, his voice high and wheezy. He added suspiciously, "Can I see some identification?"

"Um," Dan replied. "We're not cops."

"Well, what are ya then?"

"We're just helping a friend," Red cut in.

The fat man was huffing and puffing as he finally reached the fence. He produced a yellowed, *very* well used handkerchief from his rear shorts pocket and mopped his drenched brow. Against his better judgment he stuck out his hand. "Dan Coast," he said.

"Milton Guff," the man responded, taking Dan's hand. "I didn't see much, if that's what you were going to ask me."

"Did you hear anything?" Dan asked.

"Like what?"

"Like … a … gunshot?"

Milton rubbed his hand through his thinning greasy black hair and wiped crud and bits of dandruff across his lower belly leaving a stain on his shorts. "Oh yeah! Now that you mention it, I did hear something. It was like a loud pop. I thought some kid lit off a firecracker or something. I looked out my kitchen window," Milton pointed to the window facing the road, "but there was nothing out here."

"The truck wasn't sitting here when you looked out?" Red asked.

"Nope, it was a good fifteen minutes before I looked up again and noticed the truck on my sidewalk. I heard a car squeal around the corner and when I looked up, I seen the truck sitting there."

"Did you get a good look at the car that *squealed* around the corner?" Dan asked.

"Oh yeah! It was black," Milton answered.

"Did you notice the make or model?" Dan asked.

"Nope."

"Did you notice if it was a two or four door?" Red asked.

"Nope."

"But … ya got a good look at it?" Dan said.

"Oh yeah! It wa—"

"It was black," Dan said.

"Yup."

"Then what happened?" Red asked with a wide grin.

"Well, I seen that the driver's side door was open but I didn't see anyone inside. I figured whoever was driving had broken down and left in the other car with a friend or something. So just to be a Good Samaritan I thought I would run out and shut the door for them. That's when I seen the guy's legs dangling out of the door. I tell ya, I almost shit myself when I seen that guy lying across the seat like that, blood all over his chest. I thought he was dead. I ran back in the house and called 911."

"The cops said there were drugs in the car," Dan said leadingly. "Did you see anything like that?"

"Oh yeah! Right in the passenger side floor, three or

four plastic bags about yay big." Milton formed the shape of a brick with his hands. "There was a box of donuts too … the box of donuts was *already* open."

"Okay," Dan said. He reached in his pants pocket and pulled out a business card. "If you think of anything else could you just give me a quick call?"

"Oh yeah! I'll sure do that." Milton started to waddle back to his house when he stopped and turned back toward Dan and Red. "Ya know, you two boys sure asked a lot more questions than that cop did."

"What did *he* ask ya?" Red asked.

"He just asked me if I saw who shot the guy." Milton responded.

"And you said 'nope?'" Dan asked.

"Oh yeah!" Milton replied.

Dan and Red turned and made their way back towards Dan's car. "Are you thinking what I'm thinking?" Dan asked.

"I sure am. I bet that fat bastard ate one of those donuts."

"Are ya shittin' me?" Dan blurted out.

"Well, why else would he have said the donut box was already open? I bet he's the one that op—"

"Forget about the goddamn donuts for Chrissakes. I'm figuring Phil was shot somewhere else, somewhere close by. That's why ole Milty heard the gunshot fifteen minutes earlier. They dumped him and his truck here and took off in the black car."

"Well yeah, I was thinking that *too*," Red said matter-of-factly.

Chapter Sixteen

Dan and Red drove from one end of Riviera to the other. They passed a small hotel, where Red asked, "Do you think he saw something at that hotel?" and Dan replied, "Who knows."

They drove by a bank, at which point Red pondered, "Ya think he witnessed a bank robbery or something?" to which Dan looked at him over his Ray Ban aviators and responded, "Don't ya think we would have heard something about a bank robbery?"

"Probably," Red agreed.

Dan took a left on to Seventeenth Street and headed toward Flagler. When he came to Flagler he made a left.

"Maybe we ought to head over to the police station and talk to Rick," Dan said.

"Talk about what? You know he's gonna be pissed when he finds out you're snooping around." Red warned.

"Hey, we're just two of Phil's friends wanting to know what happened. All we did was ask a guy a couple questions and he answered them. No harm, no foul."

"It's your call." Red picked up a small white paper bag off the floorboard and opened it. "There's one more donut in here. You want it?"

Before Dan could answer Red had already sunk his choppers into the glazed donut. Dan rolled his eyes. "I guess not."

Chapter Seventeen

When Dan and Red arrived at the Key West Police Station they went directly to Chief Rick Carver's office. After a short wait Rick invited them in.

Rick put down his pen and with the same hand picked up a coffee mug that read WORLD'S GREATEST COP, took a sip, and set it back down on the desk. "What can I do for you gentlemen today?" he asked, leaning back in his chair and rubbing his large belly with both hands.

"Well," Red began, "we had a bet going. I said *you* were the world's greatest cop, but *Dan* disagreed. He says it's Joe Friday."

Carver didn't seem amused. He glanced down at his mug. "Joe Friday is dead, so now it's me. Now, why are ya here?"

Dan wiped the grin from his face and said, "Actually, we were on our way to lunch and we thought you might like to join us, maybe talk a little bit about Phil Lambert shooting."

"Emily packed me a lunch this morning," Carver answered, pointing to the small refrigerator on the other side of his office.

"And it all fits in there?" Red deadpanned.

Carver shot Red a look and in his best no-nonsense Southern cop voice said, "Watch it, asshole."

Dan had to hand it to Rick. He had his Rod Steiger, *In the Heat of the Night* act down pat. Or was it Carroll O'Conner he was doing? "We talked to a guy that lives over on Riviera. He said he heard what could have been a gunshot yesterday morning."

Carver gave Dan a condescending grin, leaned back even farther in his chair and clasped his fingers behind his head. "Dan, Dan, Dan," he said. "When are you going to learn to leave the *po*-leese work to thee *po*-leese? You got a guy who may have heard a gunshot? Well, I got a guy who actually saw the shooting."

"Someone saw the shooting?" Dan asked, surprised.

"That's right, Danny boy. Guy out jogging. He said Lambert's truck and a light blue Taurus sped by him on Riviera Avenue. The Taurus forced Lambert's truck up on to the sidewalk. The guy jumped out of his car and when Lambert opened his truck door the guy put a bullet in him."

"Why would someone just force Phil off the road and then shoot him?" Red asked.

"You let us worry about that. Now if that's all you boys wanted," __Carver motioned toward the door__ "I've got a lot of paperwork to do."

Dan started to leave but first asked, "What was the guy's name that saw the shooting?"

Irritated, Carver shuffled some papers on his desk. When he found the name he looked up at Dan. "And why would I be telling you his name?"

"I just want to ask him a few questions … it's for

April, Rick."

"His name is Max Drescher, but if I get one call from this guy telling me that you were harassing him I'll have you both in the slammer. Ya got it?"

"Got it," Dan said, reaching into his pocket and pulling out another business card. "Can I use your pen?"

Carver threw him his pen. "You got your own business cards now?" he asked, shaking his head. "Or in your case, *I-can't-mind-my-own-business cards*." Carver chuckled at his own joke.

Dan wrote down Max Drescher's name on the back of his business card. "You got his address?"

Carver exhaled wearily through his blubbery lips and shoved police blotter under Dan's nose. "I should have my head examined for playing along with you, Coast. He rents a little trailer over on United Street. Here's the house number."

Dan copied the address on the business card, placed it back in his pocket and tossed the pen on Carver's desk. "Thanks, Rick," he said. "I owe ya one."

"You owe me a thousand. Now get the hell outta here, both you clowns!"

"We're getting'," said Dan.

Once outside, Red climbed over the passenger side door of the Porsche and plopped down into his seat. "Are we really going for lunch or were you just saying that?"

Dan couldn't believe his ears. "You just ate four donuts for Chrissakes!"

"I know, Daddy, but it's almost noon," Red whimpered.

"Fine, we'll get lunch but then we gotta find this Max Drescher guy. He's obviously lying to Carver. We know

Phil wasn't shot where they found him, and we know there was no blue Taurus."

"Mind-your-own-business cards, that was pretty funny," Red said as Dan spun the tires.

Chapter Eighteen

Dan pulled into a parking lot across from a small trailer park on United Street.

"The sign says *for customer parking only*," Red pointed out.

"It's the phone company, Red, we're both customers."

Red chuckled, "Oh yeah, I guess we are."

Red set what was left of his large chocolate Frosty on the floorboard and climbed over the door. "When are ya gonna get that freakin' door fixed?"

Dan ignored the question and they walked together across United Street. Dan held the business card with the address in the palm of his hand. They walked through the gate of a chain link fence along a thin blacktop driveway. Small stones crunched under their flip-flops.

The driveway split into two different directions, meeting again at the other end of the trailer park. Dan chose the path to the right. They read each house number until they came to the one they were looking for. The trailer was small, probably two bedrooms. The light salmon colored paint, badly faded and warping in places, looked like it had been applied with a dirty mop and barely hid the original color, which Dan judged was horseshit green.

Dan led the way down a dirt path past an old rusted Weber grill and two white plastic lawn chairs. The lawn chairs were stacked on top of one another and Dan could see that the chair on the bottom had a busted leg. There was a mossy wooden deck that ran half the length of the trailer with the steps being at the far end. Dan went up the steps first. Red stopped on the second step.

Knock, knock, knock. Dan's knuckles rapped the thin steel door. He waited quietly; there was no answer. He knocked once again. There was movement coming from the trailer this time but still no answer.

Bam, Bam, Bam. Red pounded his fist impatiently against the side of the trailer, shaking the tornado-bait to its cement block underpinnings. "Jesus, Red," Dan whispered, "so much for subtlety."

"What the hell do you want?" boomed a voice from inside, and then the door swung open. *"What!"*

Dan wondered exactly how a man larger than the trailer itself could actually fit inside said trailer. *It must be some kind of Doctor Who timey wimey bullshit,* he thought.

Standing before them was a man at least six and a half feet tall and weighing in at three hundred pounds. If not for the zebra print bikini underwear he sported, he would have been completely naked. His head and face were slick and clean shaven, glistening with sweat. Every square inch of the rest of him was covered in thick blond hair. He looked as though he was wearing an albino gorilla suit without the mask. He clenched his teeth and pretended to smile. "What can I do for you two gentlemen?" he asked in an all-too-calm voice.

"Are you Max Drescher?" Dan asked.

"No," the man said, and yanked the door closed.

Dan and Red looked at each other. "Holy shit," Red said, wide-eyed. "Bigfoot lives!"

"What do we do now?" Dan asked.

"Um, why don't you knock again and ask him if you can speak to Drescher?"

Dan doubled his fist and raised it to knock once more. He paused for a few seconds, wondering if it was a good idea. Before he had a chance to knock the door opened again.

"You're still here?" said the man.

"Can we speak to Ma—"

The hulking beast put one finger in the air. "Hold on," he interrupted.

He pushed the door open farther to reveal an impossibly tall and thin and chalk-white woman standing in the middle of the living room. She stood in her bra and underwear, smoking a cigarette, which she favored. She was an honest to God Virginia Slims cancer stick come to life. Even her greasy dark hair, piled in a sloppy bun on top of her head, looked like an ash that might fall at any minute.

"Honey," Bigfoot said in the same calm tone. "Could you please do me a favor and call 911? Tell the operator to send the coroner because an irritating little man and his wife"__he gave Red a disgusted look__"were just beat to death while trying to break into our home as we were making love."

Dan cringed at the makes-you-want-to-stick-needles-in-your-eyes-inducing picture of these two freaks getting it on. The woman said, "Yes, Randy," and went for the phone on the end table next to the couch.

"Oh shit!" Dan said.

Randy was quicker than Dan could have imagined. A boulder-sized fist was on its way. Dan put up his arms to block and the fist hit him in the forearm, knocking him backwards and into the porch railing. Dan grunted in pain. His opponent was moving swiftly toward him, both arms outstretched. Dan quickly rolled to one side along the railing and grabbed the porch post to upright himself. Randy didn't foresee the move and crashed through the railing, hitting the ground below with a heavy thud and a *humpf* as the air escaped his lungs.

Dan looked to Red, who was on his way around the porch. Dan grabbed a broken piece of railing, ripped it from its post, and tossed it to Red. As Randy was climbing to his knees, Red, snatched the piece of pressure treated lumber from the air and brought it down on the back of the missing link's head. Randy went limp, and partook in a dirt sandwich.

Dan opened his mouth to speak just as he heard screaming and an avocado green 1970s style phone smashed against the side of his head. He put up his arm and swung around, the side of his hand connecting with the side of Honey's head. Still screaming, she stumbled backwards into the trailer.

"Randy!" she hollered, and started toward Dan again, phone in hand and dragging the cradle across the floor.

Dan raised his fist. "Don't!" he yelled. Honey stopped. "Go back in there and shut the door and shut your mouth."

Honey didn't comply. She ran at Dan, screaming, "I'll kill you!"

Dan braced his back against the post and raised his foot in the air, catching Honey in her bony chest. He shoved, knocking her to the living room floor. He ran to the door and swung it closed. He grabbed a lawn chair and wedged it under the door handle. Honey was trapped but still yelling bloody murder.

Dan ran down the steps to join Red. Randy was moaning and groaning. "I thought you killed him," Dan said.

"I aimed for his shoulders," Red answered.

"Probably wouldn't have done the trick."

"Yeah, he dropped like a giant sack of shit."

"A giant *hairy* sack of shit," Dan added.

Sirens blared in the distance. "Crap, the cops!" Red said.

"Ya think this counts as harassment?"

Red shrugged and looked down at Randy's naked hairy butt cheeks. "Huh, I would not have guessed that Randy was a thong man."

Chapter Nineteen

Dan and Red stood in front of Chief Rick Carver's desk, shuffling their feet like two naughty schoolboys that had been caught setting off a fire alarm.

"What the hell did I tell you two? I've got a man in the hospital with a fractured skull and a girlfriend that wants me to charge the both of you with attempted murder!" Carver hollered. His face was red and a long purple vein on his forehead looked like it was about to pop.

"I doubt his skull is fractured," Red shrugged. "I didn't hit him that hard."

"Yeah, and pine is a soft wood," Dan added.

Red shook his head in agreement. "He's right. I could see if it was oak or someth—"

"Shut … up!" Rick yelled. His voice was growing hoarse.

"Randy started it," Red murmured.

Dan shook his head.

Carver stroked his thinning pate with a meaty paw.

He felt a migraine coming on. "I *know* who started it. You're lucky the guy across the street saw the whole thing or you both would be sitting in a jail cell right now. Now get the hell out of my office."

Dan turned toward the door and then back to Rick. "Do you know where that Max Drescher works?" he asked.

"Get out!"

Dan and Red obliged, double-quick.

"What now?" Red asked as they approached the car.

"I'm going home. You still have that friend that works over at the probation department?"

"Garcia. Yeah, why?"

"Give him a call and see if he wants to do us a little favor."

"What *kind* of favor?"

"See if he will look up Max Drescher. I'm betting Mr. Drescher has a record, might even be on probation for something. See if he has a place of employment and maybe we will pay him a little visit tomorrow, ask him a few questions."

"Should I bring a two by four?"

"If something works, stick with it," Dan chuckled.

"What are you and your parents doing for dinner tonight?"

"You think about food all day long, don't you?"

"I think about sex sometimes too, but lately I only get food."

"I can't imagine why that is."

Dan and Red climbed into the Porsche and sped away.

"Hey," Red asked. "Why do you think Randy called *me* the wife?

Chapter Twenty

Dan arrived home around four o'clock to find his father once again asleep in an Adirondack chair by the fire pit. The crossword puzzle, a little more filled in than the last time Dan saw it, lay on the ground next to the chair. Buddy lay sound asleep on the other side of the chair, twitching fitfully as he chased gulls, or maybe Frisbees, in his doggie dream. Dan scanned the immediate area for a half empty drink, but there wasn't one, so he went in to make one for each of them. Buddy fell awake with a start. He looked up indifferently from his spot and watched Dan as he walked up the gravel path to the back door. Sighing, the aging dog put his grizzled head back down as Dan closed the door behind him.

"Mom," Dan called out from the dining room; there was no answer. He picked up two glasses from the bar and went to the freezer and filled them with ice. While making two tequila and 7UPs he called out once again. "Mom. Hey, Mom." Still no answer. He picked up the drinks and walked down the hall to his parents' bedroom and quietly pushed open the door with his foot. The room was thankfully empty. The only thing worse than watching

Randy and Honey doing the nasty would be catching his folks *in flagrante.*

Peg's suitcase lay open on the bed. A book partially covered by one of his mother's shirts lay at the top of the suitcase. He walked over to the suitcase and, setting the two drinks on the nightstand, he picked up the book. It was a photo album covered in an off-white cloth. A cloth picture frame containing a photo of Dan and his wife Alex was integrated into the album's cover. The couple stood arm in arm, looking happier, more carefree, and blissfully in love than should be legal. It was one of Dan's favorite photographs, taken at his sister's wedding three months before Alex's death. His memory of the occasion was bitter sweet. It was the last time they ever danced together.

Dan sat down on the edge of the bed next to the suitcase and, placing the photo album on his lap, he opened it. The first picture was of Dan and Alex cutting their wedding cake. He remembered they had decided not to push the cake into one another's face. He was glad they didn't. A half-smile came over his face and he slowly turned the page. The right-hand page had two photos, one of Alex posing cheek to cheek with Buddy when he was a puppy. Alex had a huge grin and it seemed that Buddy did too. The other was a picture of Alex, a knockout in a green bikini, leaning back against the hood of Dan's brand-new Porsche.

Dan reached over and picked up one of the glasses of tequila and downed it in one swig. He closed the photo album, returned it to its resting spot, and placed the shirt back over it the best he could remember. He picked up the other glass, made his way back to the bar to refill the empty one, and walked back outside.

"Made you a drink, Dad," he said, startling his father.

Gene pushed himself back up in the chair and reached for his drink. "Hey, thanks."

"Where's Mom?" Dan asked.

Gene looked at his watch, an ancient Timex with a badly scratched crystal. "Her and Bev went for a walk."

"Want me to light a fire?" Dan asked.

"Why, are ya cold?"

"No. Rarely gets cold *here*."

"Nice," Gene said, taking a sip of his drink.

"How was the fort?"

Gene made a scornful little farting noise with his lips. "It was a fort."

The two sat quietly sipping their drinks and staring into the fire pit with no fire until they heard the sound of women's laughter approaching from Bev's backyard.

"Someone left the henhouse door open," Gene cracked.

"I heard that," Peg responded kicking the leg of Gene's chair.

"I thought I was gonna have to send out a search party," Gene kidded. "I sat here worried the whole time."

"He was sleeping when I got here," Dan said.

"He spends most of his waking hours asleep," Peg interjected.

Gene shot her a look as Dan and Bev chuckled. "When's dinner? I'm starving."

Dan shook his head. "Any chance you knew Red's mother in a biblical sense forty something years ago, Dad?"

"Why?"

"Never mind."

"Hey, how about Red's for dinner?" Gene suggested.

"Sounds good to me," Dan agreed.

"Well, I guess *that's* settled," Peg huffed, making it clear she resented not being consulted.

"Is there somewhere else you would like to go, Mom?" Dan asked.

"No, Danny. I suppose coming to the island three times in his life makes your father an expert on the best local cuisine."

Dan grinned. The cooking at Red's had been called many things but never "cuisine."

Gene grinded his palms greedily and licked his chops. "Then I guess it is settled," he enthused. "Let's go!"

Peg looked to Bev. "You wanna come with us so I have someone intelligent to talk to?"

"Sure. Let me run in and change," Bev said.

"I'm gonna take a quick shower and give April a quick call, then we can go," Dan said and sprinted for the door, drink in hand.

Dan made himself another drink on his trip to the bathroom. He set his drink down on the sink and reached in his pocket for his cell phone and the day's notes.

"Hello?" April said from the other end.

"Hi, April. How's everything going?"

"No change."

"Sorry to hear that. Hang in there. A couple quick questions: Have you ever heard Phil mention the names Max Drescher or Randy Quick?"

"No, neither name sounds familiar. Why, did they have something to do with Phil's shooting?"

"I'm not sure yet. How about, did you ever hear Phil mention the trailer park over on United Street?"

"Trailer park? Why would he mention a trailer park?"

"I don't know, April. I'm just taking stabs in the dark. If ya need anything just call. I'll talk to you later."

"Bye, Dan … and thanks for helping."

April hung up the phone and Dan picked up his drink, took a sip and set it on the shelf in the shower.

Chapter Twenty-One

"Oh, goodie! Karaoke!" Gene blurted out as the group passed a chalkboard just inside the entrance of Red's Bar and Grill.

"I don't think so," was Peg's response.

Dan grinned as visions of Gene's last attempt at karaoke played in his head.

"What do you mean, 'I don't think so'?" Gene frowned. "You don't remember the last time I sang karaoke?"

Dan interjected. "Yeah, Dad, we all remember, but *you* don't."

"Bev, you said I sang like a bird."

Bev grinned and nudged Peg. "Yeah, a pterodactyl," she chortled.

The four took their seats at a six top and were soon joined by Red.

"How are you folks tonight?" Red asked cheerily.

"Wonderful," Dan and Gene answered in unison.

Red looked from Gene to Dan. "Ya know, Dan, I always thought you were quite an original character but…"

"He's just a faint copy of the original," Gene finished.

Dan pretended not to hear. "Just get us some drinks, barkeep."

Red laughed. "Peg, what can I get you to drink? I know what the rest of these alcoholics drink."

Peg scanned the menu. "Hmm, do you have a Lambrusco?" she asked.

"No, but I have a Mascato that's pretty sweet if that's what you were looking for."

"Yes, please, and a little ice in a glass."

"Coming right up." Red bent down close to Dan's ear and whispered, "I called my buddy. Drescher is on probation for breaking and entering. He says Drescher works the night shift at the Mobil station on the corner of Flagler and Riviera Street."

Dan nodded. "A few blocks from where Phil was shot."

"Zackly," Red answered and started back to the bar.

"Yo, Red, hold up" Gene said. "What time does the karaoke start?"

Red put his hand on Gene's shoulder. "Are ya sure that's a good idea, Gene? Don't you remember the last time you karaokeed?"

Gene dropped his head back down to his menu. "Apparently not."

A few moments later Red returned with their drinks and a drink for himself. He took a seat at the end of the table opposite Dan. "You folks don't mind if I join you for dinner, do you?"

"Of course not, Red," Peg responded genteelly.

"Yeah, siddown, Red, nothing makes us sick," Gene added with a guffaw

Before too long a waitress appeared at the table with a guest check pad in her hand. Her long brown hair was tied in a ponytail and her pen was stuck behind her ear. Abiding by Red's strict no uniform policy, she wore white capris and a green sleeveless top. Her arms and shoulders were brown and toned. Her perky round breasts were small but her Victoria Secret bra was not convinced and pushed her up a cup size. She had brown eyes, but Gene didn't notice.

"How are you folks this evening?" she asked in a cutesy voice that Minnie Mouse would envy.

"Wonderful," Dan and Gene chorused once again. Dan closed his eyes and slowly shook his head.

"He tries to be like his daddy," Gene confided to the waitress. Her raucous, mile-high laugh caused heads to turn at every table in the place.

Dan looked to the other end of the table. Red's smile told Dan he was really enjoying this.

"My name is Rachel," the waitress said. "Y'all know what you would like to order?"

"I think we're gonna need a few more minutes," Dan said.

"Okay, I'll stop back in a bit. Is everyone okay on drinks?"

Gene scanned the table. "I think so, just bring me a drink every thirty minutes until I pass out and then start bringing them every forty-five minutes."

Rachel brayed like a jackass and Gene said, "And keep laughing at all my jokes it'll be reflected in your tip."

Rachel winked and shot the old man with her finger. "You got it, sweetie" she said and sauntered sexily away.

Gene's peepers were glued to her ass as she crossed the floor.

"Put your eyes back in your head, Gene," Peg said. "You have underwear older than her, and just as brown in some spots." Peg turned to Red and Bev. "He's always had this weird thing for waitresses."

Red motioned to Dan and started to speak.

Dan cut him off. "Shut. Up."

Chapter Twenty-Two

Peg carefully maneuvered the rental car into Dan's driveway. Dan was the first to exit the car. He opened the passenger side door for his father, who was slumped over in the front seat still singing Jimmy Buffett's "Come Monday." Gene went to lean against the door just as Dan swung it open and went face-first into the driveway without missing a word of the song.

"Oh my God!" Peg hollered. "Help him up!"

Peg and Bev seemed concerned, but Dan was trying his damndest not to laugh.

"Well, on that note…" Bev said and headed for her front door.

"Goodnight, Bev," Peg called after her.

"Gunite, Bedge," Gene yelled. "Sleete tight, done let da bed … bucks bite."

"Come on, Dad," Dan said, helping his father to his feet.

"I shoulda been a singer, Sonny!" Gene yelled.

Dan got his father into the La-Z-Boy and began

picking the bits of crushed stone out of his forehead.

"I always said he had rocks in his head," Peg commented on her way to the bedroom.

"Damn fine comedee … comeedier … comedy person, that mother of yours. We should go on the road. We could sing and tell jokes. Sonny and Chair! I got you, babe … I'm tired." Gene closed his eyes and sunk back in the recliner.

Dan eyed the gregarious lush that was his father, as innocent looking as a baby in repose. It was impossible not to love the old fart. "Sweet dreams, Dad."

Dan quietly opened his front door and walked out on to the front porch and sat on the steps. He pulled his cell phone from his pocket and tapped the screen a few times.

"Hello?"

"Red, it's Dan."

"I know. Your name comes up on the screen when you call."

"Yeah, anyway, whaddaya say we head over to the Mobil station and get some gas?"

"Now?" Red sounded disappointed.

Dan heard a woman giggling in the background. "Yeah, now. Why, ya got something better to do?"

"Actually … remember that babe singing the Shania Twain songs?"

"I remember."

"Well it's gonna be my bed her boots are under, *if* ya know what I mean."

"Tell her she will have to take a rain check and *come on over*, if ya know what I mean."

"Ugh, fine." *Click*.

Chapter Twenty-Three

It was a little after mid-night when Dan turned off of Flagler and into the Mobil station. He pulled his Porsche up to one of the gas pumps and got out.

"Fill'-er up," he said to Red. "I'll go in and pay, and have a look around."

"Grab me one of those hot meat stick sausage things and a Mountain Dew," Red called out.

"Yup."

"And one of those big pickles."

"Yup."

Dan entered the building, walked up to the counter, and plunked down a hundred dollar bill. "He's gonna fill it," he said, motioning out the front window.

"Sure thing," the attendant said, grabbing the bill and laying it sideways across the open cash register drawer.

The name tag on the attendant's uniform shirt said Max.

"Nice night," Dan said.

"Yup," Max responded, glancing out the window.

Dan had instantly gotten a mental picture when he first heard the name Max Drescher. Now face to face with him, he saw he was not far off.

Max was in his early thirties. His thick blond hair was slicked back tight to his scalp and he had skin the color of notebook paper. He was tall and thin with full lips and a longish face whose jagged cheekbones and lantern jaw lent him a cruel aspect. A thin faint scar, barely noticeable, ran from his right earlobe, down the cheek, to the cleft in his chin. If Max were dressed in a German uniform he would have looked right at home as an extra, guarding the Allied troops at Stalag 13.

"Working nights must be boring," Dan observed, trying to keep the small talk going.

"A little."

"How late they make you work?"

"Two."

Just then a ding sounded and both men's eyes went to Red, who was placing the nozzle back in its cradle.

"Forty-two, thirty-four," Max said, picking up the one hundred dollar bill and placing it under the drawer. He counted out Dan's change, placing it in the palm of his hand. "Thanks. You have a good night."

"You too," Dan responded as he left the building.

Red was back in his seat, watching Dan as he crossed the parking lot.

"Where's my meat stick and soda?"

Dan climbed into the car hurriedly. "Oh, crap. You should have said something," he answered with mock regret as he sped away.

Chapter Twenty-Four

"Why are we at Kmart?" Red asked as they pulled into a parking spot in the Key Plaza.

"Ski masks," Dan replied.

"Are we going skiing or robbing a bank?"

Dan opened the car door to get out. "Neither."

Red climbed over his door. "Then why do we need ski masks?"

"Because we are going back to the Mobil station a little before two and we're going to grab Drescher on his way to his car and ask him a few questions."

"I bet *that's* harassment."

"Yeah, but I'm betting he won't call the cops because I'm sure he's involved in Phil's shooting."

"Then why the masks?"

"Just in case I'm wrong … or, just to keep one of us from being gunned down in the street like Phil."

The two men walked through the automatic doors and into the cool air conditioning of the store.

"I wouldn't think they sell a lot of ski masks in Key West," Red commented.

"I didn't think of that," Dan responded. "I just figured all K-marts sold the same things."

Dan and Red walked up one aisle and down the other. There were no ski masks in the hunting supplies. There were no ski masks in camping, or sporting goods, and not even in the isle with the other hats.

"What now?" Dan asked.

"Stockings," Red blurted out. "We'll put them over our heads like robbers."

Dan spun around and headed for women's clothing. "Good idea."

When they arrived on the stocking aisle both men stopped and folded their arms, gazing stupidly at the dizzying array before them.

"Holy shit, there's a lot of different kinds of stockings," Dan said.

"A lot of different colors, too," Red added.

"Should we get dark ones? I think he might be able to see our faces through the nude ones."

"I don't really think the color matters because in the movies bad guys' faces seem to be all squished, so it's hard to recognize them anyway."

"You're probably right," Dan agreed, and grabbed a package of Hanes Silk Reflections. "These sound comfortable."

"What should I get?" Red asked.

"You're gonna need a plus size to fit over that giant

friggin' head of yours."

"That's real funny," Red replied, picking up a package of dark stockings with a floral print. "These look nice."

"You're gonna look like a whore."

Chapter Twenty-Five

Dan took a left off of Thirteenth Street onto Riviera Drive. As he approached Riviera he pulled to the left side shoulder and parked his car next to a chain link fence and shut off the engine.

Just beyond the chain link fence six blue storage containers sat side by side. Three trailers were backed up against the loading dock of a large, white cement block building. There was a sixteen-foot sliding gate that exited onto Riviera Drive. On the gate was a sign that read, IS THERE LIFE AFTER DEATH? FIND OUT BY JUMPING THIS FENCE.

Across the street from where they were parked were houses. Dan wondered if anyone who lived there may have heard or saw anything the morning Phil was shot. Maybe they did and just didn't want to get involved.

Off in the distance a dog barked and right after a cat screeched in holy terror. *Ouch*, Dan thought. *Dog one, cat zero.*

"What now?" Red whispered.

Dan looked to his wrist and rolled his eyes. "What time is it?"

Red looked at his watch. "One-fifteen. Why don't you just buy yourself a watch?"

Dan sighed and lay his head back on the seat and stared up at the winking stars in the clear sky. "Now we wait till Max gets out of work."

Red swatted at a mosquito. "I should have grabbed some Off! at K-marts."

"K-marts?" Dan repeated. "How many K-marts were there?"

"What do ya mean?"

"It's just K-mart, singular, there's no S at the end. Read the sign next time."

"I was ending it with an apostrophe S … ya know, like to show ownership. Like that store is Kmart's store, they *own* it." Red said in a superior tone.

"Nice try."

"You're a real asshole," Red said, climbing out of the car.

"My mother's dying words."

"Your mother is still alive, dick-head."

"Yeah, but she'll probably say that."

Red walked around and sat on the hood of the car. He crossed his legs and then his arms and stared off down the street in wounded silence.

Dan thought about reaching under the seat and grabbing the bottle of tequila that was screaming his name. He wondered how Red couldn't hear it. He leaned down and touched the bottle but decided against it. He felt a small amount of shame. It was that slight bit of shame that always told Dan when he was drinking too much. He leaned back in his seat.

"What time is it?" Dan inquired.

Red didn't answer.

"What, you're not speaking to me now?" Dan asked.

"Its five minutes after the last time you asked me." Red snapped.

"Sorry for asking," Dan replied.

"Ya know," Red began without turning around. "The only reason you point out every flaw I have is so you feel better about your own fucked-up life. Dan Coast, lottery winner. Big deal! There's a lot of wealthy people on this island. What makes you so special? I don't have to be out here in the middle of the night like this. I *have* a life. I have a business to run. I blew off a sure thing tonight, and for what? To listen to you pick on me. *Jeeze!"*

"Technically its morning, not the middle of the night," Dan said matter-of-factly.

Red threw his head back and covered his face with his hands. "Are you kidding me!"

Dan, smirking, got out of the car and started walking toward the corner. "I'm gonna walk over and take a quick look in the gas station, make sure Drescher is still in there."

"I'll be here," Red said as he watched his partner round the corner out of sight.

Ten minutes later Dan returned, a can of Mountain Dew in his hand. He tossed it to Red. "Here, I grabbed you a soda out of the soda machine."

Red caught the Dew, opened it and took a big drink.

"You're welcome," Dan whispered to himself and walked over to the gate in the chain link fence. He put his fingers through the chain links as he looked inside the yard and gave the gate a hard tug. It was locked up with a thick chain and a pad lock.

"What is this place?" Dan asked Red.

"Um," Red said, looking around to get his bearings. "I think it's a place that sells boat parts or something. I think they have clothing, fishing supplies, things like that. Hey, it's almost two, should we get ready for this thing?"

Dan opened his car door and put his knee on the driver's seat. Leaning over and opening the glove box he pulled out a small roll of duct tape and a Beretta 92FS 9mm Inox. He looked at the inscription on the barrel: *Buon compleanno figlio mio.*

"What does that say," Red asked.

Dan looked up to see Red standing at the passenger door. "Who knows?" he said and placed the gun in his waist band at the small of his back.

"Is that our old friend Jimmy P's gun?" said Red, referring to a blast from their mutual past, a Mafioso who figured prominently in another of Dan and Red's amateur sleuthing.

"It was, now it's mine."

"I gotta get *me* a gun," Red complained.

Dan reached into the Kmart bag and pulled out two packages, tossing one to Red. They each used their teeth to open their package. Red pulled out his first.

"Crap!" Red said. "These are pantyhose."

"So?" Dan responded, pulling his from the wrapper.

"You got any scissors?"

"For what?"

Red pulled his pantyhose over his head. "To cut off the other leg."

"Just tuck it in your shirt."

"Good idea," Red said. "Now what's the plan?"

"First I want you to jump in the car and turn it around so it's facing the other direction, a complete three-sixty as you would call it. Then I want you to wait right here at the corner. I'll walk down and hide behind the dumpster and grab Drescher as he's walking to his car. I'll walk him back this way toward you. You join us and together we'll walk him all the way down this street to the dead end at the canal. We'll get him behind the bushes down there," Dan pointed to the end of Riviera Street, "and ask him a few questions."

"Sounds good," Red agreed, climbing into the Porsche.

Dan, stockings in hand, disappeared around the corner once again. When he was almost to the corner he heard his car start. He looked back and saw Red doing a U-turn in the intersection.

When Dan reached the large green dumpster he squatted down behind it, pulled out a stocking, pulled it over his head, and waited. Dan sat quietly wondering which of the two cars in parking lot was Max Drescher's. He could see the gas pumps where he waited; there were no customers. He heard a car engine cruising to a stop and saw headlights. He pushed his back up against the dumpster and peeked around it. A bald Hispanic man, shaped like a giant pear and wearing a uniform shirt just like Drescher's, exited the car. The man disappeared around the corner of the building. Seconds later a bell sounded as the man entered the gas station.

Dan waited for what seemed like another eight or nine minutes. The bell sounded again and Max Drescher walked around the corner of the building. He was feeling in his pants pocket for his car keys and whistling a tune.

John Jacob Jingleheimer Schmidt, Dan thought. *His name in my name too.*

Just as Drescher slid his key into the keyhole of his dark brown 1979 Plymouth Duster he felt Dan's hot breath on his neck and cold steel behind his right ear. Drescher froze.

"Please … please, my wallet is in my back pocket. Please don't kill me," Drescher quietly pleaded.

"Just do as you're told and you won't get hurt," Dan promised, his voice husky and menacing through the stocking.

Drescher shook his head and sniffled. Dan could tell that Drescher was crying. *Good God,* he thought. *For someone who looks like a Nazi, he's sure a pussy.*

"Put your hands behind your back," Dan ordered.

Drescher did as he was told. Dan put his gun back in his waist band, pulled the duct tape out of his cargo shorts and wrapped it four times around Drescher's wrists. Dan spun him around and walked behind him to where Red was waiting at the corner.

Drescher took one look at Red's dark floral print panty hose and broke down. "You guys are gonna do some sick sex shit to me aren't you?"

"No," Red protested in disgust.

Dan grinned. "I told ya you'd look like a whore."

The two men escorted Drescher to the end of the street and told him to get on his knees behind some bushes. Dan took one look around to make sure there was no one watching. He pulled out his pistol and laid it on Dreschers shoulder.

"Please don't kill me! I did everything you told me. I never said a word to anyone," Drescher cried.

Dan and Red looked at each other and then back at Drescher. "What exactly did we tell you to do?" Dan asked.

Drescher sobbed. "The story, the story I gave to the cops ... about seeing the shooting ... and ... and the blue Taurus."

"That wasn't us." Dan pushed the barrel of the gun harder into Drescher's shoulder. "Who told you to lie to the cops?"

"I don't know."

Dan smacked the gun against the side of Dreschers head just enough to get his attention. "Who?" Dan asked.

"I swear I don't know. I've never seen them before."

"What did they look like?" Red asked.

"One guy was tall, a white guy. He had real short hair, and an accent, almost like Russian or something. The other guy was dark-skinned and a little shorter, big muscles. He was in charge, he told the little guy what to do. He had a tattoo on his arm, a dragon, or a snake or something."

"Why you, Max? How did they know you?" Dan asked.

"I stopped over at work that morning to pick up my paycheck. I forgot to grab it the night before. On my way out, Raul, that's the guy who relieves me, asked me to take out the garbage for him. While I was putting it in the dumpster I heard something going on over there at the parts place around the corner. When I walked over I see the taller guy loading this other guy into a truck. I started backing away so they wouldn't see me but the other guy grabbed me from behind. He pulled out a gun and made me go over by the truck. He told me to wait around till the cops got there and he told me what to say. He put the gun up to my head and told me that he would be back if I didn't do exactly what he told me. I thought you guys were them coming back to kill me."

"This is your lucky day, Max." Dan reached down and ripped the tape off of Drescher's wrists. "Now jump in the canal."

"Wh ... what?"

"You heard me, jump in."

Drescher stood up and quickly did as he was told.

Red looked over the edge at Drescher treading water. "Now swim to the other side and count to a thousand before you swim back ... or we'll be back to do some sick sex shit to ya."

The duo was still laughing as they got back to the car. "What now?" Red asked as he climbed in.

"Stop asking, 'What now'," Dan started the car.

"Well you never let me in on the plan."

Dan popped the clutch and spun the tires. "What plan? There's no *plan*. We're just playing it by ear. Why don't *you* come up with a plan?"

"Well, first we could stop and get something to eat."

"It's almost three in the morning," Dan pointed out.

"What time did your mom tell you to be home?"

"Shut the hell up."

Chapter Twenty-Six

When Dan Coast awoke Tuesday morning at nine twenty-three, he was in his own bed, he was wearing his own pajama bottoms, and he didn't have a hangover. He could smell breakfast cooking again for the second morning in a row. Sausage this morning, and something else, maybe home fries.

Dan rolled over from his stomach to his back and laced his fingers behind his head. He could hear Buddy snoring on the floor at the foot of the bed. Dan cleared his throat and Buddy jumped up and got comfortable in bed next to Dan. He reached over and scratched the mutt behind the ears. "How ya doin, fella?" Dan asked. Buddy looked at his master and put his head back down and closed his eyes.

The door to Dan's bedroom was open and he could hear movement and conversation coming from the other room. He picked out his father's voice, and his mother's, but there was another person too, a woman. Dan listened for a while and then it came to him; Edna Mcgee, from across the street. *I wonder what the old busybody wants,* Dan thought.

Dan swung his legs over the bed, got up and went to his dresser for a T-shirt. He grabbed the one on top and held it out in front of him. BOILERMAKER 2005, the shirt read. He remembered that day. He finished that race in ninety minutes; Alex finished it in eighty-four. He folded the shirt back the way it was and placing it back in the drawer, he grabbed a plain black T-shirt and slipped it over his head.

"What's all the commotion out here?" Dan kidded as he walked into the dining room.

"Good morning, Danny," Edna said. "I brought you some Christmas cookies."

Dan looked to the table at the big aluminum tray filled with several different kinds of cookies. He pulled back the green plastic wrap and reached for a cookie. Peg slapped his hand. "After breakfast," she said. "And did you tell Mrs. McGee 'Thank you'?"

Dan stroked his smarting hand and gave his mother a look. "What am I, ten years old? Thanks for the cookies, Edna."

"You're very welcome, Danny. It's the least I could do, what with everything you do for me around my house."

Peg got up from the table and went into the kitchen. Dan quickly grabbed two cookies and shoved them into his mouth. Edna gave him a great big smile.

When Peg walked back into the dining room she handed Dan a cup of coffee and kissed him on the forehead. "How did you sleep?"

"Good Mom."

"Ya got in pretty late," Peg said.

"Three in the morning," Edna added disapprovingly.

Dan rolled his eyes. "You two would make good spies."

"You're lucky to have people who worry about you," Peg said. "Can I get you another cup of coffee, Edna?"

"No, thanks, Peg, I better get home. I have about ten more plates of cookies to deliver," she answered. Edna got up from the table and walked toward the door.

Before she went out the door, Peg called out, "Oh, Edna stop over Christmas Eve, we're going to have a little get together. Nothing too big, about nine or ten people, some eggnog, some Christmas music, you know, the usual."

Dan glared at his mother as she spoke to Edna. When she finished talking and Edna left, he was still staring.

"What? It will be fun," Peg assured him.

"No, it won't," Dan said quietly.

"You *love* Christmas."

"No, Mom, I *loved* Christmas." Dan said as he walked with his cup of coffee out the back door, down the gravel path to the fire pit.

It was a cool morning and Dan thought about building a fire. He thought about how relaxing it would be to sit and stare into the fire as he drank his cup of coffee. He looked over toward the small wood shed that sat in the back corner of his yard. He heard his back door slam.

"Should we build a little fire?" Gene asked.

"Sure, Dad, that would be great."

Gene went back inside and soon returned with the newspaper from the day before. Dan got up from his seat, went to the woodshed and grabbed four pieces of firewood and laid them by the pit. Dan knew not to interfere with Gene's fire building. He learned that long ago as a child

115

while camping with his family at Piseco Lake or Nick's Lake in the Adirondacks. When they went camping Gene built the fire, Gene made the breakfast, and Mother did everything else.

Dan sat back in his seat and watched as Gene worked his magic. He remembered his father's rule: *One match, Danny, one match. It should never take you more than one match to light a campfire.*

Gene separated each page of the newspaper and crumpled it into a little ball, stacking each ball one at a time into the fire pit. When the newspaper was gone he looked at the wood Dan had brought him, got to his feet, and walked to the shed to search for kindling. When he returned to the fire pit he stood each piece of kindling on end around the paper in the shape of a teepee. Then he did the same with the larger pieces of wood. Gene reached into his pocket and pulled out a book of matches. He lit a match and held it to the paper, smiling as it caught. He touched three more places and they also caught fire. Within seconds the whole fire pit was ablaze. Gene blew out the match.

"One match, Sonny," Gene said holding up the smoking match.

Dan smiled. There was still something about watching his father build a fire that impressed him and made him feel like a kid again.

The screen door slammed again. This time it was Peg bringing Dan a plateful of eggs, sausage, toast, and home fries.

"Just in time for *breaktist*," came Red's voice from behind Dan.

"Good morning, Red," Peg said with a smile. "Can I make you some eggs?"

Red grabbed a lawn chair leaning against the shed.

"You sure can, Peg, thanks." Red unfolded the aluminum lawn chair and placed it between Gene and Dan. "Nothing smells better than a morning fire."

"And eggs and sausage," Gene added.

"It's funny how you always happen to show up right at mealtime," Dan said.

"Yeah," Red said. "It's like I got a *sick* sense or something."

When Peg had gone back inside and out of ear shot Red turned to Dan. "I didn't sleep at all last night. I laid there all night waiting for the cops to break in my door and arrest me."

Gene uncrossed his legs and leaned forward. "Why, what did you two boys get yourselves into last night?"

"Nothing," Dan said. "We just went and questioned a guy about Phil's shooting."

Gene looked dubious. "At one o'clock in the morning?"

"The guy didn't get out of work till two," Red explained.

"You couldn't have questioned him *before* he went to work?" Gene argued.

"No, this had to be done in the dark," Red laughed.

"I don't even want to know," Gene said throwing his hand in the air.

"I don't think Drescher is in any position to talk to the cops." Dan assured Red.

"I was worried about someone else calling the cops," Red said. "I could hear Dresher yelling for help as we pulled away. Someone else might have heard him too. Someone screaming for help at two in the morning is a little attention getting."

"I didn't hear a thing," Dan said. "You probably imagined it."

"I hope so," Red replied.

Chapter Twenty-Seven

It was a little after noon by the time Dan showered and made it to the hospital. April had called; Phil had taken a turn for the worst, she explained. Dan went directly to Phil's room but he wasn't there; neither was April. The nurse on duty wouldn't give Dan any information about Phil but she did tell him that April was in the cafeteria.

Dan sat in a white plastic chair across from April at a white Formica-topped table with metal folding legs. A paper cup of coffee sat in front of April and a red plastic tray with a half-eaten salad had been pushed to her right. Her purse sat on the floor at her feet. The cafeteria was just as cold and surgical feeling as the rest of the hospital, with the exception of floor to ceiling, wall to wall windows with a great view of the parking lot.

"Do you want a cup of coffee?" April asked, keeping up a brave front.

"No thanks, I think I'm about coffeed out for the day. My mother won't stop filling my cup every time it hits the half-way mark," Dan answered.

April grinned. "It must be nice having them here for the holidays."

"Yeah … I guess."

April sat silent for a few moments.

"So … what are the doctors saying?" Dan asked.

"He's got an infection, so they had to open him up again," April answered staring out the window.

Dan reached across the table and put his hand on top of April's. "He's going to be fine, Ape."

"That's what I keep telling myself." She paused for a moment. "He's all I have Dan."

Dan knew exactly what that meant; he knew exactly how it felt. When that one person you build your whole life around is suddenly gone, you have nothing, nothing but memories. The memories that you once cherished become a constant painful reminder of what you lost.

After a few moments Dan changed the subject. "We talked to a few witnesses about the shooting."

"Witnesses?" April asked.

"Well they didn't actually see the shooting, but one guy said he heard what could have been a gunshot about fifteen minutes before he saw Phil's truck out his kitchen window. The same guy said he saw a black car speed away from Phil's truck. We also talked to another guy that admitted he was paid five hundred bucks by two guys he had never seen before to say he saw the shooting. They also told him to say he saw a blue Taurus speed away from the scene."

Dan now had April's full attention. "Did you find out who the two guys were?" she asked.

"No."

April looked disappointed. "Did you tell Chief Carver about the two guys?"

"No. I figured there wasn't any sense in it. He's got the witness that lied and said he saw the shooting and he's concentrating all his efforts on the drugs they found. Once he gets an idea in his head I'd damn well better have a lot more to give him before he changes his mind."

April nodded in agreement. "It's you I trust, Dan. You do whatever you think is best."

"The one question in this whole thing is: What was Phil doing over there? Why was he on that side of the island?"

April shrugged. "I don't know."

"Think, April. What did he say before he left? Was he in a good mood, a bad mood? What was the conversation that morning?"

April's head slowly turned back to the window. Dan could almost see the wheels inside turning as she tried to recall that morning. "He *wasn't* really in a good mood that morning, I remember. He was … complaining … because Derrick was supposed to be back from Chicago two weeks ago and he had two jet skis that needed work. He was also angry because he had ordered a part for the boat, it was supposed to be in last week but it hadn't come in yet. I don't know, Dan, it was pretty much business as usual. There's always something broken down, there's always a part on order. The only thing that's different is that Derrick is usually here to deal with it."

Dan grinned. "Yeah, Red is really missing Cindy too."

"I bet," April smiled back. "You know, Dan, nothing was going right for Phil that morning. First he couldn't find a pen to write down a phone number he had looked up. I've showed him a hundred times which drawer I keep the pens in. He finally gets a pen and he had forgotten the number, so he had to look it up again. Then on the way out the door I noticed a big stain on his ass, he must have sat in something. He had to come back in and change. By the time he left he was pretty pissed." She sat quiet for a minute. "He always says I love you before he goes out the door, but he forgot that morning."

The two sat together taking turns looking up at the big plain-faced Elgin clock on the wall. Dan had wanted to leave, but decided to stick around until there was some word on Phil.

"How long has he been in surgery?" Dan asked.

April looked at the Elgin once again. "About forty-five minutes."

"Did they say how long it should take?"

"They didn't say."

Dan stood. "I think I *will* grab a cup of coffee. You want another one?"

"Yes, thanks."

As Dan made his way toward the coffee machine he reached into his pocket for his money clip. *Shit*, he thought, reaching into his empty pocket. He spun around. "It looks like you're buying, April. I left my money clip in my other pants." He stopped dead in his tracks. "Uh, hey, Ape …"

April was unzipping her purse. "Yeah?"

"What did you do with Phil's pants?

"His pants?" April looked confused.

"The pants with the stain."

"As usual *he* just threw them on the bedroom floor, so *I* picked them up after he left and put them in the hamper. Why?"

"Did you check the pockets?"

"I don't remember, but I usually check pockets right before I throw them in the washing machine."

"Give me the key to your house."

"Why, what are you thinking?"

"I'm thinking that on a morning where nothing was going right maybe he forgot the number and left it in his pants pocket. Maybe the number had something to do with where he was going."

"Mrs. Lambert," came a voice from the doorway.

Dan and April looked over to see a nurse. Instinctively they both tried to read her face. Did she have good news, or bad news? *I would not want to play poker with this nurse*, Dan thought.

"Yes," April answered.

"Your husband is out of surgery."

"Is he okay?"

"He's in recovery right now. He will be there for a few hours, probably, then they will move him back to his room in the ICU."

"But is everything *okay*?"

The grim nurse was immune to April's unease. Dan figured she had starch in her veins.

"You can follow me to recovery to see him. His doctor will be there in a bit to talk to you."

The nurse turned and went out the door with April hurrying to keep up with her. Before disappearing down the hall she yelled back to Dan, "There's a key hanging on the wall to the right just inside the garage door!"

Chapter Twenty-Eight

April failed to mention that the garage door was locked. Dan went from one window to the other; they were both locked as well. Then he went to each of the house windows. *Locked, dammit!* Every television show he had ever watched, in which the main character broke into a house, ran through his mind. *Credit card!* He reached into his pocket. *Shit!* No wallet.

Dan walked back to his car and opened the trunk; there was a screwdriver, some rope, a roll of duct tape, and a roll of thick clear plastic. *Nothing to help me break into a house, but I'm all set to abduct someone,* Dan thought. He grabbed the screwdriver and returned to the window in the back of the garage, where he hoped no one would see what he was about to do.

When he got to the window, he took the screwdriver by the shank and smashed the window with the handle. He kept hitting the glass until he had made a hole big enough so that he could reach his arm through and unlock the window. With the window unlocked, he opened it and went through head-first landing, on the concrete floor with a thud. As Dan made his way to where April said the key would be hanging, he heard a car door bang shut. He looked out the garage door window. It was Red. Whistling off-key, he walked up the driveway, turned, and made his way up the walkway to the front door; he turned the knob and went in.

Dan could feel his face redden and his blood pressure rise as he looked down at his hand and the small puddle of blood that was forming on the floor beneath it.

Dan walked over to Phil's tool bench, picked up the cleanest rag he could find and wrapped it around his bleeding hand.

Red heard the garage door opening and walked back outside. "What are ya doing in there," he asked Dan.

"Looking for the key to the front door," Dan replied.

"It was unlocked."

"Oh, really?" Dan said as he brushed past Red and into the house.

"Hey, did you know your hand was bleeding?"

"No, Red, I hadn't noticed.

"So why did you want me to meet you here?" Red asked.

"I guess I'm a glutton for punishment."

Red looked confused and shrugged his shoulders as he walked to the refrigerator and opened the door.

"What are you doing?" Dan asked.

"I'm thirsty. I was seeing if they had a soda or something." Red reached in and grabbed a can of Diet Pepsi. "Ugh, diet! I would rather drink elephant piss," He opened the top and took a big drink.

"Just make yourself right at home."

Red's window-rattling burp showed that he intended to. "So, what are we doing here?"

Dan leaned against the countertop. "Throw me one of those sodas." Red tossed him the can. Dan opened it and took a sip. "April said Phil wrote down a phone number on a piece of paper and stuck it in his pants pocket, and then he changed the pants before he left. I was wondering if the number was still in there." Dan pushed himself away from the cabinet and walked into Phil and April's bedroom.

Red noticed the phone book lying on the counter; he opened it and slowly went through the yellow pages.

"Crap!" Dan called out from the bedroom.

"What's the matter?" Red yelled back.

"Pockets are empty."

When Dan returned to the kitchen he saw Red bent over the countertop, gently rubbing a pencil back and forth across a note pad. "Now what are you doing?" he asked.

Red slid the note pad over to Dan, in the pencil marks Dan could make out a faint phone number.

Red grinned. "You're not the only one who watches old detective shows."

"Nice job, Rockford," Dan said as he took the pencil from Red and copied down the number on another sheet of paper. "Now we just have to find out whose number this is."

Red took out his cell phone. "There's an app for that." He looked at the number and typed it into his phone. He stared at the screen and after a few seconds said, "Flagler Marine."

"Phil was checking to see if the part he had ordered for the boat had come in. What's the address?"

"Thirty-two, twenty-four Flagler," Red replied.

"That's right near the Mobil station," Dan pointed out.

Red put his phone away, walked over to a cupboard and opened the door. "Awesome," he said. "I haven't had a Twinkie since they brought them back."

"I find that hard to believe."

Red picked up the box, reached in and pulled one out. He slowly waved it in front of Dan's face. "You want one?" he asked slowly.

"No."

Red opened the clear plastic wrap. "I wonder if they still taste the same." Red stuffed half of the Twinkie into his mouth and bit down. "Oh … my … God!" he exclaimed. "I think they are even better."

Dan ripped the box from Red's hands. "Okay! Give me a friggin' Twinkie!"

Chapter Twenty-Nine

"Ugh," Red moaned. "I don't feel so good."

"You ate a whole goddamn box of Twinkies. What did you expect?" Dan asked.

"I didn't eat a whole box, *you* ate one of them."

Dan took a left on to Flagler. "You're like a damn goldfish. You just keep on eating until the food is gone … or you explode."

"The Pepsi was a diet."

"Oh well, that's good. The diet soda probably cancels out the chunks of white lard wrapped in a greasy yellow sponge. When the world finally goes to shit from a nuclear holocaust or whatever, the Twinkie shall inherit the earth. Those things are indestructible. I bet you've got fifty pounds of undigested Twinkie in your frickin' colon, for Chrissakes."

Red said lamely, "Well, you ate one."

"Yeah, *one*," Dan said as he pulled into the parking lot of Flagler Marine. He shut off the engine and got out of the car.

"The Mobil station is right next door," Red said.

Dan nodded. "Yeah, probably not a coincidence."

The two men walked up to the front door. The sign stuck to the glass said OPEN but the door was locked. Dan pressed his forehead against the glass and shaded his eyes to look inside. The place was empty and the lights were off.

"What do you see in there?" Red asked.

"A whole lotta nothing," Dan responded.

Dan jiggled the door one more time just to make sure and then headed toward the gas station.

"Where are you going?"

"I'll be right back, wait here."

Dan walked across the parking lot of Flagler Marine, hopped over a twelve-inch cement curb and disappeared into the front door of the Mobil station. "Excuse me," he said to the young man behind the counter.

The young man's name tag said SKIP. With his shoulder-length, sun-bleached hair and vacuous expression, Skip was a dead ringer for Jeff Spicoli, the pot-addled surfer in *The Fast Times at Ridgemont High*, a flick Dan very fondly remembered for two reasons: One, Phoebe Cate's auspicious in-the-buff debut, and two, the tall thin blond he brought to the movies to see it.

Dan could hear a repetitive pounding coming from the fluorescent green ear buds jammed into the young man's skull. Skip bobbed idiotically his head while reading an article on extreme skateboarding in the dog-eared copy of *Juice* magazine.

"Excuse me," Dan said again.

Skip still didn't hear. His mind was light years away in a land where minimum wage guys who rode skateboards to work are kings.

Dan reached out, took hold of the two wires dangling from Skip's ear buds, and gave a quick yank.

"Yo! Dude, wadja do that fer?" Skip whined.

"Yo! Dude," Dan responded. "I'm looking fer the guy who owns the store next door."

Skip pointed out the window. "There *is* no store next door, dude, that's just the street."

Dan rolled his eyes and pointed in the opposite direction. "The other next door, the boat parts store."

"Oh, yeah … that store. That old dude ain't been there in a few days. He usually comes over in the morning, like, for coffee and a newspaper. Nice old dude. Ya know, he was in a war or something. It's guys like him that made it possible for guys like us to live like we live."

"Guys like us?" Dan asked.

"Yeah, you know, regular dudes?"

Dan reached into his pocket and pulled out a business card and handed it to Skip. "If you see anything strange going on over there or anyone you don't know, can you give me a call? Ya know, us regular dudes gotta stick together."

Skip took the card and gave Dan the thumbs up. "You know it, dude."

Dan turned toward the door. "Thanks, Skip."

"Whoa, dude, how did you know my name?"

"It's on your shirt, dude."

"Oh right." Skip quickly looked at the business card he was holding and pointed at Dan. "You got it, Dan."

Dan walked back over to Red who was leaning against the car with his arms folded in front of him.

"Find out anything?" Red asked.

"Well, *duh*," Dan said in his best surfer accent. "The old dude that owns this place has been totally A-W-O-L for a few days, and I also learned that the old dude was a bitchin' war hero who fought for our right to talk like this."

Red looked confused. "Ohhh*kay*."

Chapter Thirty

Dan drove Red back to April and Phil's house to pick up his car. After dropping Red off he called April.

"How's he doing, Ape?" Dan asked.

April sounded discouraged. "He's back in ICU. The doctor is saying the same thing he said the day they brought him in: 'The next few days are crucial.'"

"Crucial?" Dan asked.

"I guess that's their way of saying if he lives through the next few days he may live a few more."

"Have you had any sleep at all?"

"I've dozed off a few times in the chair but not really."

"April, you should go home for a while ... take a shower ... get some rest," Dan insisted.

"I don't want to leave him here by himself. What if he wakes up and I'm not here?"

Dan could hear the heartbreak in April's voice. "Yeah, I understand. Hang in there, honey." He hung up as he took a left off of Ashby Street on to Sky View. As he slowly drove down the street, he could see Noah riding his bike. Dan pulled to the curb, stopped, and watched as Noah rode his bike down the driveway into the street, making a large circle, and then riding back up his driveway. He would then turn around in his driveway and start the loop all over again.

Dan pulled away from the curb and stopped in front of Noah's house. Noah smiled big when he saw Dan.

Dan spoke first. "What's up?"

Noah stopped his bike, jumped off the seat, and stood straddling the bike. "Nothing."

Dan noticed Noah's bike had a downward curving crossbar. "Is that your bike?"

"Yeah … it's a *girl's* bike."

"I see that."

"The people who lived here before us left it. It's okay though. I can't ride a boy's bike very well anyway cuz the straight bar makes it so I can't reach the ground."

Dan's eyes went to the wooden blocks duct-taped to the pedals. "Your dad put those on there for you?"

"No … my mom, so I can reach the pedals."

Dan smiled. "Good idea."

"My dad doesn't live with us anymore. Him and my mom fight too much, so he had to leave."

"Oh, that's too bad. Where does he live now?"

"I don't know, but the police said he can't come here anymore."

Dan reached in his pocket and pulled out a business card. "Noah, my name and number is on this card. It's my cell phone number. You stick this in your pocket and when you go in your house you hide it somewhere in your room. If you ever need me for anything, you call me."

Noah took the card and looked at it. "Need you for what?"

"Anything. If you need help, or you just want to talk about anything, you call me."

Noah shrugged his shoulders and put the card in his pocket. "Okay."

"Noah!" Dan turned to see a gray-haired woman across the street making her way down her front steps. "Noah, is everything okay?"

"Yes, Mrs. Fields," Noah called out.

The old woman approached Dan's car. Dan shut off his engine and got out.

"This is Dan, Mrs. Fields. He's my friend."

Dan stuck out his hand. "I'm Dan Coast, I liv—"

Mrs. Fields cut him off. "Noah, why don't you run over to my house? There's fresh baked cookies in the cookie jar. Turn the TV on something you want to watch."

"Dan made some boys quit pick—"

"Noah, go in the house." Mrs. Fields said.

Noah jumped back on his bike and started across the street. "Okay. Bye Dan."

"Bye, Noah," Dan said. He stood with his hand out but Mrs. Fields didn't take it.

Mrs. Fields was five foot short, around seventy years old, and weighed in at about ninety-eight pounds soaking wet but the steely-eyed glare she was giving made Dan feel a little nervous. She walked around the car and moved in close. Dan took a step back.

"What's your story?" she barked.

"Um, I'm Dan Coast?"

"Are you asking me or telling me?"

Something in her voice told Dan she may have been a retired Army drill sergeant. "I *am* Daniel Coast, ma'am," he said slowly. "My friends call me Dan."

"And?"

"And I live over on Beach View Street."

"And?" Mrs. Fields raised her hand to scratch her head and Dan flinched.

"And I was driving home the other day and saw some boys picking on Noah. I stopped the car and chased them away and gave him a ride home."

"That was nice of you, young man. Thank you," Mrs. Fields said. Her pursed little mouth curled into something like a smile and she firmly shook Dan's hand, which, in his terror, he had never put down.

Dan exhaled; he didn't realize he had been holding his breath. "What's the story on Noah's dad?" he asked.

"Probably shouldn't tell you this, but I will," Mrs. Fields began. "Noah and Jeanie moved in here about a year ago by themselves. A couple months later, Carl, that's Noah's father, moves in with them. Seems he was in prison up in Raiford. He wasn't here a month before the screaming and yelling started. The cops were over there at least once a week. About three months ago, he beat poor Jeanie up pretty bad. She was in the hospital for four days. Noah stayed with me; they don't have any kin around here. Jeanie got a restraining order against the bastard, pardon my French, and he spent thirty days in jail. Haven't seen him since."

"Now I can see why you're so protective of Noah," Dan said.

"Now you're catchin' on. He spends a lot of time at

my house. His mother works two jobs just to make ends meet, what with Noah's medical bills and all."

"Medical bills? Because he's a midg__, I mean, a little person?" Dan asked.

"No, no. Noah has a heart ailment, cardio … hyper … something-or-other. Something with a long name."

"Jeez, he looks fine."

"Looks fine, acts fine most of the time. He gets tired a little easier than most kids. He's a good boy."

"They're lucky to have someone like you living right across the street."

"I do what I can. Well, I better get on back in the house," Without a word of goodbye Mrs. Fields spun on her heels and was gone.

Dan climbed back in his car and started the engine.

Mrs. Fields got about halfway across the street and turned around. "Young man!" she called out.

"Yes, Mrs. Fields?"

"Don't think I didn't see you staggering through my yard the other morning like some drunken hobo." Mrs. Fields pointed to her eye and then at Dan.

Chapter Thirty-One

As Dan Coast pulled into his driveway he noticed that his parents' rental car was gone. He walked along the gravel path that led from his driveway to his backyard. Gene was not at his station in one of the Adirondack chairs by the fire pit. He walked through his yard and into Bev's, up her steps and onto her deck. Buddy lay in front of the back door.

"Where is everybody?" Dan asked the mutt as he bent down to scratch his head.

Buddy said nothing. Dan reached out and knocked on Bev's screen door.

"Bev!" Dan hollered through the screen.

"I'll be right there!"

Dan stood and backed up to one of the picnic table benches and sat down. Buddy got up and walked over to Dan laying his head on Dan's lap. He wasn't ready for the head scratching to end. "How come you don't go lay over in your own yard?"

"He likes me better," Bev answered for Buddy through the screen.

"He's a great judge of character," Dan agreed.

"I was just going to make myself a cup of coffee," Bev said. "Can I make you one?"

"Sure, that would be great. Make mine with tequila, hold the coffee and add a little 7UP."

Bev grinned. "Maybe I'll make mine with rum then."

As Bev went to make the drinks, Dan stretched out on the bench and looked up. Cotton candy clouds were scudding lazily across the blue sky. The sun was hot but not too hot. *Ahhh.* "You need a hammock out here."

"I bought one and a frame for it a couple weeks ago. It's still in the box," Bev hollered back.

"Why didn't you say something? I would have put it together for you."

"I didn't want to bother you during the holid—" Bev stopped.

Dan knew what she meant. *Great, everyone I know thinks I'm helpless through the holidays.*

Bev back-pedaled. "I mean … I, uh …"

"I know what you meant, Bev, I'm not an idiot."

Dan sat up on the bench as Bev walked through the back door with the drinks. She handed one to Dan. "I'm sorry, Dan I just—"

"Bev, it's all right, don't worry about it. Do you think I don't notice that everyone I know acts like they have to walk around on eggshells this time of year?"

"Hey, at least I didn't call your parents, right?"

"What do you mean, call my parents?" Dan asked.

"I mean … uh …" Bev took a quick drink of her rum and Coke. "I didn't mean anything."

"Bev, did someone *call* my parents?"

Bev jumped up. "Well I have a lot of housework to do."

"Did Red call my parents and tell them to come down here, Bev?"

"I don't know."

"Ya look like you know something."

"Dan I'm sorry, it slipped out. Don't be mad at Red," Bev pleaded.

"So it was Red."

Bev shook her head. "Yes."

"What an asshole." Dan took a sip of his drink and put his head down.

"He did it because he worries about you. We thought tha—"

Dan looked up. "We?"

"He came to me a few weeks ago with the idea, and I agreed with him."

Dan finished his drink, put the glass on the picnic table and got up. "A conspiracy," he whispered as he walked down the steps. "We'll talk about this later. Oh, and the reason I came over here is because I wanted to see if you would run over to the hospital and sit with Phil for a little while so April can go home and get some rest."

Bev finished her drink. "Sure, I can go over right now."

"Thanks, Bev." Dan walked down the steps and back to his house. As he reached his yard he looked back and called for Buddy. The old mutt lifted his head, looked at Dan and then followed Bev into her house. *Man's best friend.*

Chapter Thirty-Two

Dan stood next to his dining room table; he was talking on the phone. "I need it the day after tomorrow."

"Sir, that's Christmas Eve! We couldn't possibly get you one by Christmas *Eve*," said the voice at the other end.

"Your web page says guaranteed delivery in two days," Dan argued.

"We do guarantee delivery in two days, but we also need a couple days to build it. These are all custom built, sir."

"I'll pay double … triple, whatever it takes."

There was a long pause at the other end. "I've got something here that someone else ordered and then canceled on me. With a few hours' work I could probably turn it into what you're looking for, but it's green not blue."

"Green would be fine, thanks a lot."

Dan gave the man his address and phone number and hung up just as Gene and Peg walked through the front door.

"Hey, Sonny!" Gene called out.

"Hey, Dad. Where have you two been?"

Peg answered as Gene made his way to the recliner. "Well, first we went to the Earnest Hemingway house."

Gene interrupted. "You know, Danny-boy, some of his cats still live there."

Dan stood at the bar making his father and himself a drink. "Wow, sixty-year-old cats! That's pretty impressive."

Peg spoke up. "Gene, those were *descendants* of Hemingway's cats."

Gene looked confused. "Oh, I thought those cats were actually his cats." He gave Dan a wink. "An' some of those cats have thumbs."

"Oh, don't be stupid, Eugene," Peg said. "Cats don't have thumbs."

Dan laughed out loud. "For once he's right, Mom. Some of those cats do actually have six toes. I've seen 'em: They look like they're wearing mittens."

Peg shook her head. "Really?"

"Really!" said Dan and Gene together.

"Well, you never know with him. Half the time I think he's lost his mind. Last week I put the nursing home on speed dial."

Dan handed Gene his drink. "Do you want a drink mom, Mom? You look a little stressed."

"You try spending the day with him! Everything that comes out of his mouth is foolish."

Gene grinned. "Yeah, I'm a moron."

Peg started down the hall. "I'm gonna lay down and take a nap."

"We also took a ride on the Cock Train."

"*Conch* Train!" Peg yelled from the bedroom.

Gene and Dan quietly laughed amongst themselves.

Gene picked up the remote control from the end table. "You need a couch or something, or at least another chair."

"I know," Dan replied. He grabbed a dining room chair and put it next to Gene and sat down.

Gene flipped through the channels and stopped on an old repeat of *The Andy Griffith Show*. "Oh I love this one. It's the one where Barney thinks someone is robbing the armored car carrying a gold shipment but it's actually the Feds using it as a decoy."

"That probably would have been funny," Dan replied.

Chapter Thirty-Three

Dan opened his eyes; it was dark in the room except for the glow of the idiot box. *Andy Griffith* had now been replaced by an old episode of *Rosanne*. Dan's legs were outstretched and crossed on the floor in front of him; his arms were crossed and resting on his belly. He sat up straight and moved his head from side to side cracking his neck. He knew it was a mistake to fall asleep in a dining room chair and he was almost scared to stand up. His back was tense and his shoulders ached. He tried to stretch each part of his body. It's always good to stretch before a rigorous workout and these days getting out of a chair you had fallen asleep in was quite a workout.

The creaking of the wooden chair woke up Gene. "What's the matter?"

"Nothing, just getting up."

"To make another drink?"

"You want another drink?"

"I thought you would never ask!" Gene handed Dan his glass.

Dan walked to the freezer with both glasses and filled

them with ice. When he returned to the dining room his mother was exiting the hallway. "Still drinking?" she sighed.

"It's our second drink; we both fell asleep in our chair."

"*Sure*, and cats have thumbs."

Dan shrugged and made the drinks. As he handed Gene his drink his cell phone rang.

"Hello?"

"Yo, dude, guess who this is."

"Skip," Dan replied.

"Awesome, dude, how did you know?"

"Lucky guess. What's up?"

"Hey remember when you told me to call you if I saw anything bogus going on around that old dude's store?"

"I remember."

"Well I did."

There was a long pause as Dan waited for Skip to continue. "What?" he finally asked.

"What, *what*?" Skip asked.

"What did you see?"

"Oh, yeah. I went out to get something out of my car and heard someone yelling for help, real quiet like, so I start walking over where it was coming from, ya know, to be a good samolian and what-not. Because like, if some dude is in troub__,"

"Skip! *Focus*."

"Oh, right, sorry dude. So I start walking over there all Ninja-like and when I get to the fence right behind one of those big storage trailer thingies, I hear someone pounding on it an' yelling 'help, help!' So I start to climb the fence and this black car comes driving up. So I jumped back down on the ground. This big Ivan Drago dude gets out of the car and unlocks the gate."

"Ivan Drago?" Dan asked.

"Yeah, you know, *Rocky IV*. 'I must break you,'" Skip said slowly in his best Russian accent. "He even talked like that too."

"The other guy, was he smaller and dark-skinned?" Dan asked.

"Whoa, dude, you must psychic!" Skip said. "So this Drago dude walks over to the storage trailer, opens it up and goes in, then he comes back out dragging the old dude that owns the store. Dragos saying, 'I thought we told you to keep quite or we would quiet you permanently.' The old dudes saying, 'you bastards better kill me now or I'll kill you later.' That old dude wasn't scared or nothing. Drago smacked him around a bit and then threw his ass in the car and sped off."

"How long ago did this happen?" Dan asked.

"Like fifteen minutes ago."

"Did you call the police?"

"No, you told me to call you."

"Oh … right. Well don't call them, I'll be there in a half hour."

"Roger that. I get out of work in a few minutes but I'll hang around till you get here. Later, dude."

Dan hung up his phone. "Dad I gotta go check on something. I'll be back a little later."

"Maybe I'll just come with you," Gene said climbing out of the La-Z-Boy.

"I don't think that's such a good idea, Dad."

"Why, is it something about the case you're working on?"

"Yeah, and I don't know exactly what we might be walking into. It could be dangerous, Dad."

Gene laughed. "Sonny, I was in Vietnam."

"Dad, you were a jet mechanic."

"They gave me a gun."

"Do you have one now?"

"No, why, can I get one?" Gene asked, his eyes wide.

"No you can't get one, Christ."

"You got one?"

"Yeah, I got one."

"Then I feel safe, let's go."

Dan rolled his eyes. "I'll leave a note for Mom." Dan went to the kitchen and grabbed a piece of paper and pen out of a drawer and brought it back to the kitchen table.

"What are ya gonna put in the note?" Gene asked.

"How about, 'Hey, Mom, taking Dad out to get him killed. Be back soon.'"

"Ha-ha, yeah, write that!"

Chapter Thirty-Four

Dan and Gene drove slowly down Riviera Drive. Dan shut off the headlights and coasted to the side of the road at the rear of Flagler Marine. It was dark, darker than it should be. Dan looked up at the streetlights; the one directly behind Flagler Marine was out.

"What are you looking for?" Gene asked.

Dan pointed at the streetlight. "Kind of convenient, don't ya think?"

Gene walked over and stood directly under the light. "It's broken; looks like someone threw a rock at it or something." He kicked at the broken glass that lay at his feet.

"*Psssst.*"

Dan and Gene looked around and then at each other.

"*Psssst.*"

"I think someone sprung a leak," Gene said.

"Come on out, Skip," Dan quietly called into the darkness.

Skip came out from his hiding place around the corner. "Roger that, dude."

"What the hell are you hiding from?" Dan asked.

"Someone was here and left just before you guys pulled up," Skip answered.

"They came back?"

Skip shook his head. "No, it was a different guy, a *really* big dude. He pulled up and parked right where you're parked now. He got out of his car and went in the store through the back door." Skip pointed at the back of the building.

"What did he look like?" Gene asked.

"I couldn't tell, it was too dark."

"What kind of car was he driving?" Dan asked.

"I couldn't see it from where I was hiding. Like, I just heard it pull up and heard the dude get out of it and then I could see him between the storage thingies when he walked by."

Dan looked over at the three large orange storage bins that lined the chain link fence bordering the Mobile station. "Which storage unit did you hear the pounding coming from?"

"The one in the middle, dude, right there," Skip answered pointing at the unit.

Dan motioned toward the fence. "Come on, Dad let's have a look inside. Skip, you stay here and warn us if anyone is coming."

"Roger that, dude. Should I do a bird call?" Skip cupped his hands around his mouth. "Caw, caw, that's a crow. Or should I do like a cat, meow, meow?"

"How about if you just whisper loudly, 'Hey, dudes, there's someone coming.'"

Skip gave Dan the thumbs up, "Roger that, dude!" he said and went back to his hiding place.

Dan, followed by Gene, jumped up on the six-foot high chain link fence and hoisted themselves over one at a time, dropping to the ground on the other side. Dan got to the storage unit first, Gene limped up behind him.

"What did you do, Dad?" Dan asked looking down at Gene's feet.

"Nothing, why?"

"You're limping."

"No I'm not."

"Yeah you were. You hurt yourself jumping over the fence, didn't you?"

"No," Gene said, jumping up and down. "See, I'm fine," he said wincing slightly.

"Mom's gonna kill me if anything happens to you, so be careful!"

Gene replied. "Roger that, dude."

Dan returned his attention to the storage container. "Its pad locked," he said lifting the lock and chain that was weaved through the door handles.

"Hold on, there's some pipe over here," Gene said. He walked over to a piece of two-inch galvanized pipe that lay on the ground and picked it up. When he returned to the storage container, he lifted the pipe over his head and brought it down on the lock busting it open.

"Learn that in Vietnam, didja?" Dan joked.

Gene dropped the pipe and grabbed the chain yanking it off of the door handles. Dan pulled the door open.

"Shit!" Dan said.

"What?" Gene asked.

"We should have brought a flashlight."

"Un momento, por favor," Gene said. He pulled his truck keys from his pants pocket and handed them to Dan. "Ta-da!"

Dan looked at the keys. There were three different key chains hooked together holding at least twenty keys. At the end of one ring was a small LED flashlight.

"Why do you have all these keys with you? You didn't even drive here, and … you have a rental car."

"Ya know, Sonny, you sure ask a lot of dumb questions. A real man never leaves the house without his keys."

"And I'm not a real man, I suppose?"

"Just use the flashlight, for crying out loud … oh and there's a can opener on there too, if ya need one," Gene replied with a wry grin.

"Gee, thanks."

Dan pushed the button at the end of the flashlight and the storage container lit up. The two men cautiously entered. At the far end was a blanket and pillow. Scattered about on the floor was a few potato chip bags, a couple empty soda cans, and a half-eaten box of saltine crackers.

"Looks like somebody was forced to squat in here for a while," Gene remarked.

"Sure does," Dan agreed. "Probably the owner of this place. Surfer boy said he hasn't seen him in a few days."

When Dan and Gene felt they had seen all there was to see in the storage container they exited and closed the doors wrapping the chain back around the handles and replacing the busted lock the best they could.

"What now, Sonny," Gene asked.

"Hold on," Dan replied, running up to the back door

of the store. A few security lights were lit inside and Dan scanned the store for anything unusual. He thought about breaking the window and going in, but thought better of the idea when he noticed the green flashing light coming from the security system keypad. He walked back to where his father stood. "Let's get out of here, Dad."

When the two men were safely back on the other side of the fence, Skip came out of his hiding spot. "The coast was clear the whole time, dude."

"Thanks, Skip, "Dan said. "Why don't you go ahead and take off. You need a ride anywhere?"

"No, dude, that's my car right over there," Skip answered pointing at a canary yellow mint condition 1974 Volkswagen Thing, parked where Max Drescher's car was parked the night before. The backseat was crammed full of skateboarding and surfing paraphernalia. Looking like a Jeep with a glandular condition, Dan thought the Thing was probably the most aptly named vehicle of all time.

"Sweet ride, dude," Gene said as he turned and went back to the Porsche.

"Thanks, old dude. Wanna catch a ride with me?"

"Uh, no," said Gene, "I'm good."

Dan rolled his eyes. "And Skip let's not mention this to anyone, okay."

"Roger that," Skip replied turning toward his car. "Later dudes."

Chapter Thirty-Five

It was almost nine o'clock when father and son climbed up on the orange vinyl bar stools at Red's Bar and Grill. Gene looked around the room as he waited for the bartender to take his order. He looked at the bamboo that lined the front of the bar. He looked at the Landshark Lager and Red Stripe neon signs that hung on the wall.

"I love this place," Gene said. "It reminds me of one of those bars in that movie with Tom Cruise and that Austrailian guy, Bryan somethingorother."

"*Cocktail,*" Dan answered.

"Bryan Cocktail?"

"No, Dad, the movie was called *Cocktail.*"

"No, the one where they flip the bottles in the air while they're making the drinks."

"Yeah, Dad, that was Cocktail."

"No, I don't think so, that don't sound familiar."

"Whatever."

"Hey! What can I get for you gentlemen?" Red

shouted as he walked through the kitchen door.

"I'll have the seafood platter and a whiskey and ginger-ale," Gene quickly responded.

Dan looked at his father. "We're eating?"

"I am," Gene replied as he grabbed the drink that was sliding his way.

"What about Mom?"

"It's almost nine, I'm sure she's already eaten."

"New York strip and fries," Dan said.

Red wrote down the orders, made Dan his usual tequila, Seven, and lime, and went back to the kitchen. When he returned to the bar minutes later, he made himself a drink. "So, what brings you two out tonight?"

Gene took a sip of his drink. "Running down some clues."

Red looked surprised. "Without me?"

"It's bring your father to work day," Gene kidded.

"Ya still could have called me," Red sulked.

Dan shook his head and took a sip of his drink. "It was a spur of the moment thing. Skip, the kid from the gas station, called and said he saw the same two guys that talked to Drescher. They were out back of the boat parts store."

Gene added. "Yeah, the kid said they took some guy out of one of those storage containers and drove off with him."

"We think it was the guy who owns the store," Dan put in.

Red's head bobbed back and forth from Dan to Gene as they told their story.

"And then another guy came back to the store a few minutes before we got there … a big dude," Gene said.

When Gene and Dan finished their tale, Red's only response was, "Well you could have swung by and picked me up."

Dan rolled his eyes and slid his glass back across the bar. "Fill'er up," he said.

Red grabbed the bottle of tequila in one hand and the soda gun in the other and proceeded to make Dan's drink.

"Red,' can you flip those bottles in the air like Tom Cruise?" Gene asked.

"No," Red answered, and then turned to Dan. "So, what's next?" Red slid the glass back to Dan.

Dan hooked a thumb at Gene. "I say we take Rambo home and then you and I go back to the storage containers, find a good hiding spot, and stake out the place."

"Awesome, a stakeout!" Red said.

Gene looked a little hurt. "I want to go on a stakeout. I never been on a stakeout before."

"I doubt Mom would want me taking you back there. We'll be out there all night," Dan said.

"What you call hell, I call home," Gene argued.

"Hey, catchy, I like that! said Red. "You just make that up?"

"On the spot," said Gene.

"No he didn't!" said Dan. "That's from *First Blood*. And you're still going home, Dad."

"Okay, okay, I'll go home but if something goes down, you might wish someone with my military expertise was there."

Dan grinned. "If our jet breaks down, we'll call you."

Chapter Thirty-Six

Dan drove his Porsche down Flagler Avenue. Red was flipping through the stations on the radio.

"Just pick a station," Dan said as he took a right-hand turn onto Eleventh Street.

Red ignored him. Dan took a left onto Riviera Drive.

"Oh, great song," Red said stopping on Phil Collins singing "In the Air Tonight."

As they rounded the corner Dan looked over at Milton Guff's house; the lights were on. "I wonder if old Milton is married," he said.

Red paid no attention to Dan; he was eagerly anticipating that way-cool drum breakdown.

They left Milton's house behind and slowed down a little as they got to the back of Flagler Marine and then drove as far as Seventeenth Street before turning and making their way back onto Flagler.

As they drove down Flagler, Red commented, "This reminds me of that first episode of Miami Vice."

"I hope not," Dan responded. "The bad guy got away in that episode."

Red pooched out his lips and nodded. "That's right, I forgot about that."

Dan turned his car into the parking lot of an office supply store right next door to Flagler Marine and eased into a spot next to the sidewalk facing the street. Just as Dan climbed out of the car his cell phone rang.

"Hello?" Dan said.

"Dan?" a young voice whispered.

"Yeah, who is this?"

"My ... my Dad's here."

"Noah?"

The phone went dead.

"We gotta go," Dan said, spinning back toward the car.

"What's wrong?" Red inquired.

"I'll tell you on the way."

Both men jumped back in the car. Dan started it and spun the tires as he drove over the sidewalk, jumping the curb and hitting the street doing forty. Goggle-eyed, Red was desperately searching for his seatbelt.

Dan ran two stop lights and three stop signs before pulling up in front of Noah's house. As he pulled up he turned off the lights and the engine and coasted to a stop. He reached over Red's legs, popped open the glove box, and grabbed the Beretta. "You knock on the front door then hide around the side of the house," he ordered Red. "I'll go through the back door. If any guy other than me comes out that front door, kick the shit out of him."

"Gotcha," Red replied and moved toward the front door.

Dan, gun in hand, ran down the side of the bungalow, glancing in each of the four windows as he ran by. There was light coming from each window he passed but he saw no signs of anyone. When he reached the back porch, he quickly but carefully climbed the steps. The rear light was on. Dan reached up and unscrewed the bulb. He tried the doorknob; it was unlocked, and he went in. He made his way across the kitchen floor to a doorway that led to the dining room. He paused and listened.

Dan heard a woman's voice coming from upstairs. She was crying and pleading, "Please, Mel, please don't hurt him!"

Then he heard a man's voice, obviously drunk, his speech slurred. "Where are you, you little bashtard? Our life wush great till that little freak came along."

"Mel, no!"

Dan made his way up the stairs; each step creaked from his weight. When he got to the top of the stairs he looked both ways down the hall. At the far end of the hall a man came out of a room; a woman he recognized as Jeanie from the liquor store was grabbing at his shirt, trying to pull him back inside. Dan sized him up. He was a run of the mill, muscle-bound loser with too many tattoos and chips on both shoulders. Everything about the man, his wolfish eyes, his mean gash of a mouth, his my-shit-don't-stink swagger screamed slime-ball.

The man turned and smacked the woman upside the head with the back of his hand, hollering, "Get offa me you schtinkin' bitch!" She fell back into the room. Dan noticed the knife in the man's hand as he turned around and went into the room across the hall.

Dan made his move. He ran down the hall and looked

through the doorway. The woman was getting to her feet. She looked at Dan and he put his finger to his lip. "Stay in here," he whispered. Dan quietly closed the door and went after Noah's father.

When Dan stepped into the room, Mel was standing in front of the closet door bouncing the knife back and forth from one hand to the other. "Come out, come out wherever you are!" Mel sang.

Dan walked up behind Mel and whispered, "Hey, Mel…"

Mel turned around. "What the fu—" Dan viciously smashed the pistol barrel into the side of Mel's head. Mel dropped to his knees and the knife slipped from his hands, clattering across the hardwood floor.

Dan grabbed the stunned man by the hair with one hand as he pointed the gun at Mel's head with the other. "Come on, asshole, let's take this outside. We don't want any women or children getting hurt … or seeing how bad you are about to get hurt."

As Dan was dragging Mel through the bedroom door, Mel clawed at the door jambs like a cat being put into a bathtub. Dan brought the butt of the gun down on Mel's fingers forcing him to let go. As they went out into the hall Dan looked back. He could see Noah looking out from under the bed. He was smiling. Dan gave him a wink and kept on dragging Mel down the hall, down the stairs, through the dining room, into the kitchen, and out the back door.

As the two men reached the back porch, Mel stood and tried to run. Dan kicked one of Mel's feet behind the other, tripping him. Dan grabbed him by the collar and dragged him down the steps. He shoved him face first into the dirt and ground his foot on the back of Mel's neck. Mel spluttered and cussed with his mouth full of dirt.

"Taste good, asshole?" said Dan before taking his foot off.

Mel rolled over and wiped his mouth with his bony wrist. "Big man with a gun," he shouted.

Just then Red trotted around the corner of the house and down the driveway. Dan handed Red the gun.

"Go put this back in the glove box," Dan said.

Red took the gun from his friend and slipped it into his waistband. "I think I'll just keep it right here, if you don't mind."

Dan turned back to Mel. He put both hands out in front of him, palms up, and flexed his fingers in a challenge. "I don't have a gun now," he said slowly, evenly.

Mel lowered his head and charged at Dan, hitting him in the solar plexus with his shoulder and driving Dan backwards into the side of the house, knocking the wind out of him. Dan dropped to his knees, gasping for air. Mel stepped back and landed a roundhouse kick to the side of Dan's head. Dan's eyes flashed white as he hit the ground. Mel raised his other foot to stomp on Dan's head. Dan rolled out from under his opponent's foot and quickly got to his feet. A trickle of blood ran down from the corner of Dan's mouth. He felt dizzy and wobbled a bit.

Mel gave him no time to rest and quickly came in for round two with both fists swinging like a windmill. Dan stepped aside and stuck out his foot, tripping him. As Mel was on all fours trying to get up, Dan gave him a kick in the ribs. Mel grunted loudly as he collapsed on his side. Dan steadied himself and followed through with a kick to the face. Mel's nose exploded.

Dan stepped back and let Mel get to his feet. "You broke my nose, you son of a bitch, you broke my nose!" Mel shouted as he staggered blindly in mortal agony.

"We're just getting started," Dan said with a smile and dealt Mel a right to the jaw and a left to the eye. Mel stumbled backwards but remained upright.

By this time porch lights all over the neighborhood were coming on and people were gathering at the end of the driveway. Dan looked at the crowd and then back at Mel, who was coming in for more. Dan gave him a right to the stomach that doubled him over. Dan grabbed the back of Mel's head and yanked it down and slammed his knee into Mel's face. When he let go of Mel's hair he dropped to the ground like the sack of shit he was. The crowd cheered.

"We better get out of here," Red said, but it was too late, the sound of sirens were already piercing through the once peaceful night.

Dan held out his hand for the pistol, and when Red handed it to him he took it straight to Mrs. Fields, who had been watching the fight from the sidewalk. "Here," Dan said. "Take this gun and hide it in your house. I'll come for it tomorrow."

Without a word, but the barest hint of a smile, Mrs. Fields took the gun from Dan and tucked it into her gray cardigan and went back to her house just as the first patrol car arrived.

Dan looked over to see Noah and his mom coming down the front steps. Noah ran up to Dan and threw his tiny arms around his legs. "I knew you would come, Dan. I told my mom you would save us."

In the glare of the street lamp Dan could see the bruise on Jeanie's cheek already turning purple and starting to swell. She smiled bravely. Dan thought her dimples were as beautiful as ever.

"We meet again," she said.

"Didn't think you would remember me."

"Sure I do, and I'll never *forget* you, now. Noah told me how you came to his rescue with those bullies. You were already his hero, and now—"

"Look, Jeanie, I'm not one for hearts and flowers—"

Jeanie quickly put a hand on his cheek. "You know what, Dan?"

"What?"

"You do have a good one, all right," she said softly. "A good heart."

Chapter Thirty-Seven

"Jail, what do you mean you're in jail?" came Gene's confused voice from the other end of the cell phone.

"Dad, just listen! I only have one phone call," Dan answered.

"I'll be right there."

"No, wait, listen, go in my bedroom and pull back the carpet in the closet, there's a couple loose floorboards, pull them up. Underneath the floorboards is a black duffle bag. Open it up, there's cash inside. Count out ten grand and bring it down for mine and Red's bail money."

"Roger that, dude, I'll be there as quick as I can."

Dan was shaking his head as he hung up the phone.

"What's the matter?" Red asked.

"My father keeps talking like Spicoli."

Red raised his eyebrows in a question.

"You know. Sean Penn. The surfer dude in *Fast Times*."

Red shrugged. "Whatever, dude. Is he coming to bail us out?"

"Yup, he'll be here as quick as he can."

*****

It was a little after ten AM Wednesday morning when Gene came walking down the hall, grinning from ear to ear. "Well, well, well, what do we have here?"

Dan stood at the front of the jail cell, his arms dangled limply through the bars. He fantasized about having a tin cup to rake across the bars to irritate the "screws." He glared at Gene as he sauntered down the corridor. A police officer seated at a nearby desk quickly put away his cell phone and stood as Gene approached the prisoners.

"I take it these rowdies are yours," the cop said.

"The one in the front there," Gene said, pointing, "that's my little pride and joy."

The officer laughed as he took a large key ring off of a hook near his desk. "You must be very proud."

"A chip off the old block," Gene chirped.

The officer made his way to the cell, stuck the key into the lock, turned it, and slid open the bars. Dan pulled his arms back through the bars and called to Red, who was seated and sound asleep at the back of the cell on a bench. "Come on, Sleeping Beauty, our ride is here."

Red opened his eyes and slowly got to his feet.

"Let's go, children, daddy is here to pick you up," the officer said.

"Everybody's a comedian," Red griped as he walked past the guard.

When Gene, Red, and Dan walked through the door at the end of the hallway, Chief Rick Carver was there to greet them. He stood with his legs slightly spread and his beefy arms crossed and resting on his belly. Like always, his aviator sunglasses were tucked into the front of his shirt.

"Sorry about this, Gene," Rick said, "but your son and his sidekick seem to think it's okay to run around town beating the tar out of people."

"Mel started it," Red said.

Rick ignored Red's comment; he had heard it all before. "This makes two people that these two morons have put in the hospital in less than a week," he added.

"The guy had a knife, Rick," Dan argued. "I saw him hit his wife, and then he went after the kid. What was I supposed to do?"

Rick's meaty hand shot in front of Dan's face. "*The guy* is in custody, Dan. He's going a way for a long time after what he did last night."

"Then why are ya yelling at us? It sounds like we did the right thing."

"Because I'm sick and tired of you two A-holes running around this island trying to do my job for me. Keep your nose in your own business. Now, both of you, get the hell out of my police station, and don't leave town, remember, you have a court date coming up."

"Where would we go?" Dan whispered as the three men made their way out of the police station.

Coasts of Christmas Past

As they got to Gene's rental car, a brand-new blue Ford Focus, Gene offered. "Come on you two convicts, get in the car and I'll buy you both some breakfast."

Chapter Thirty-Eight

Gene walked into the house first, followed by Dan. They had eaten breakfast and then dropped Red off at his house. Gene walked immediately to the bar to make a couple of drinks. Dan walked into the room with his head down. He was a grown man, but nothing made you feel more like a child than to have your father pick you up from the police station and then listen to the third degree from your mother when you got home.

Peg and Bev sat at the dining room table, a cup of coffee in front of each of them. Bev was making a valiant effort to hide her amusement. Peg, on the other hand, was not the least bit amused.

"Yeah, make a drink," Peg said, her anger becoming very clear. "That's exactly what you need."

"It's for sonny," Gene responded. "He's had a rough night."

"I would imagine *most* of his rough nights are *caused* by alcohol."

"Mom, you don't understand," Dan said.

"I understand more than you think I do."

Coasts of Christmas Past

Dan began telling his mother the story of the young boy picked on by the other kids and about the drunken father who had broken into the house to harm him and his mother. He ended his story with the immortal *what was I supposed to do* line. His mother didn't buy into it. She was more worried about her own son than someone else's. Her face was red and her eyes were misty.

Peg, dabbed her tears with a Kleenex and collected herself. She fidgeted with her coffee cup and then fixed Dan in an icy stare. He knew he was in for the lecture to end all lectures.

"Maybe it's time you started worrying about your own life and stop butting into other people's," she began. "You're my only son, what if something was to happen to you? You run around drunk half the time getting into trouble, and it's always someone else's trouble. You've been in two fights since we've been here. And last night, what was that? Some kind of payback for everyone who picked on you when you were a kid? You don't eat right or take care of yourself! You go from one woman to the other, trying to find a substitute for what you lost. There is *no* substitute, Daniel. You can't replace her, but if you stop acting like an asshole and get your act together maybe you might find someone. It's time to move on. I … *we* … want you to be happy. Things have to ch—" Peg threw her arms in the air. "Oh, damn it all to hell! Forget it, I'm done."

She bolted from her chair and stalked down the hall to her bedroom, slamming the door.

Bev slowly got up from the table. "Uh, guys, I'm gonna head on home."

Gene and Dan were silent. Gene walked over to Dan and handed him his drink. "I made one for myself too, I didn't want you drink alone. They say that means you might have a problem."

Dan took the drink. "Yeah, I wouldn't want anyone to think I have a problem."

The two men took their drinks to the backyard and made themselves comfortable in the Adirondack chairs by the fire pit. Gene had brought the crossword puzzle out with him and within ten minutes he had solved two clues and was sound asleep, his half empty drink sitting in the dirt by his side. Buddy had joined father and son and was lying at Gene's feet. Dan sipped his drink as he stared out at the beach, his mother's words echoing in his head.

The rest of the day was pretty uneventful. Dan sat and watched his father sleep for about an hour, even drifting off himself a couple of times. Buddy got up once to get himself a drink out of the bowl that Peg had put by the steps and then walked over and picked up an old tennis ball that lay in the yard. Buddy brought the ball over to Dan and dropped it at his feet. Dan picked it up and threw it toward the house. Buddy ran after it and fetched it back to Dan. The dog let out three sharp woofs. There was a youngish light in his eyes. Dan guessed the old dog still had some life in him after all.

The commotion woke Gene; he held his hand up in the universal sign of *throw me the ball*. Dan complied.

Gene caught the ball and climbed out of the chair. "Come on, Sonny. Let's go for a walk on the beach."

Dan got up and together they walked toward the evening tide lapping at the shore. Gene threw the ball into the ocean and Buddy eagerly went after it. Gene and his son walked along the water's edge talking idly as Buddy chased after the tennis ball time and time again, never tiring of the game.

"Your mother just worries about you all the time," Gene said.

"I know."

"She wishes you would come home."

"This *is* my home, Dad."

When Gene and Dan returned to the house they went in, made two more cocktails, and turned on the TV. Peg didn't come out of her room until dinner time. Dan asked if she would like to go to dinner. She declined and made herself and the two men each a BLT with cottage cheese and sour cream and onion potato chips. When they had finished their sandwiches, father and son asked for another. Peg did so without complaint. She was over her mad.

After dinner was over and Peg had washed, dried and put away the dishes she made the big announcement. "You guys get your shoes on. We're going to buy a Christmas tree. I'll be in the car."

Dan looked helplessly at his dad.

"You heard her, Son. Get your going britches on."

Chapter Thirty-Nine

Gene held the six-foot Douglas fir by its trunk and bounced it up and down, checking the ground for fallen needles. "This one looks nice," he said.

"Too short," Peg argued.

Dan grabbed a Scotch pine nearby. "How about this one?" he asked.

"I don't like those kind," Peg answered.

"Why not, Mom?" Dan said.

"Never mind why not."

Gene grabbed a third, a forth, a fifth, and then a sixth. "How's this?"

"Turn it around," Peg ordered.

Gene did as he was told. "Good?"

"Very nice."

Thank God, Dan thought.

They paid for the tree and the lot attendant tied it to the roof of the Ford Focus and the family was on their way.

"I wish your sisters were here," Peg said on the ride home. "This is the first Christmas we've ever been away."

"I'm sure they're doing fine without you," Dan kidded.

"As if!" Peg scoffed.

When Dan and his parents returned home Peg ordered the men to stand aside. She slid Dan's La-Z-Boy to the other side of the room and slid the TV over to the opposite wall. They put the tree in front of the window that faced the street and decorated it with the lights and bulbs that were on loan from Bev.

Gene plugged in the lights as Peg went to their bedroom. When she returned she was holding a porcelain angel in a white satin dress. Dan recognized it immediately. "I brought this from home, Danny," she said solemnly. "It was in some of the boxes you left in our attic."

Dan took the angel from his mother and stared into its lifeless eyes. His chest tightened. He rubbed his hand over the angel, straightening her dress. Dan was angry at his mother for bringing the angel, but at the same time every Christmas that he spent with Alex flooded his mind. He smiled. A tear ran down Dan's cheek, and then another, there was no fighting it. He wiped the tears away and handed the angel to his father.

"You put it on, Dad," he said.

With great ceremony Gene took the angel and placed it on top of the tree and stepped back. "I don't think I would be smiling that big if I was going to spend the next few days with that tree shoved up my ass," he said.

Dan wiped his eyes and laughed.

"Let's go out front and see how it looks," Peg said.

Peg, Gene, and Dan walked out the front door and into the street; they turned around and stared at the tree through the window. Dan's house had never looked prettier, and he said so.

"Perfect," Peg said.

Dan put his arm around his mother and pulled her close. "Thanks, Mom." He kissed her on the forehead. "I love you."

"I love you, Danny."

When they all went back into the house Gene kicked off his shoes and sat down in front of the television. "Make your old man a drink, Sonny."

Dan was halfway to the bar when Peg walked back into the room from the hall. "Put your shoes back on, Gene, you're gonna run me over to the KMarts for some Christmas CDs. We will need music for the party tomorrow night."

"Can't we just listen to the radio?" Gene replied.

"No! Let's go, Gene. You want to come along, Danny?"

"I think I'll pass Mom, thanks. I'm gonna go over to Red's and have a couple drinks."

"I think I'll pass too, Peg," Gene tried.

Peg headed toward the door. "The only thing you'll be passing, Gene, is gas. Now, come on!"

Chapter Forty

Dan climbed aboard his favorite barstool and looked up and down the bar and then around the crowded room. Red was nowhere in sight. At the far end of the bar a young woman Dan had never seen before was pouring a draft beer for a customer. The new barmaid was tall and had to bend over slightly to pull the tap handle. The gentleman sitting at the bar waiting for his beer was enjoying the show; his eyes were glued to the breasts that were pouring out of her T-shirt. He hoped this would take a while. Dan straightened his back to see if he could get a look, too.

When the beer was topped off she set the glass on the bar. The ogler guiltily raised his eyes from the cleavage buffet to meet her gaze. She smiled. She knew what he was looking at, of course, and hoped it would help with the tips. She took the man's money, spotted Dan, and approached him. "What can I get for you, honey?" she asked. She was wearing a tight dark blue T-shirt with DALLAS COWBOYS stitched in white letters across the chest, which had room for several more football team names. Beneath the lettering was a large white star. The front of the shirt had been cut from the collar down about eight inches to reveal about half a mile of expensive cleavage and expensive-looking golden-hued hooters being pushed up by a lacy blue bra. Her denim shorts were about as short as they could legally be. Dan was certain Red had hired her on the spot.

"You can get me a tequila, Seven, and lime."

"You got it, sweetheart."

Sweetheart. That was much better. "And you can just call me Dan."

"Dan it is," she responded as she turned to grab the Quervo off of the back shelf.

Dan spoke up. "Make it well tequila."

She let go of the bottle, spun around to the well, and bent over to grab a bottle of cheap tequila. *Showtime,* Dan thought as he gazed down the front of the young woman's T-shirt. She looked up and winked. Dan looked away quickly.

"Here ya are," she said, sliding the drink across the bar. "That'll be five-fifty."

Dan looked around the room again. It had been quite a while since he had paid for a drink in Red's and he didn't want to start tonight. After searching the bar he reluctantly reached into his front pocket for his money, peeled a fifty off the top and tossed it on the bar.

"Thanks, I'll grab your change."

"Keep it," Dan said.

"Um, thanks."

"Yeah, just be here when I need you."

Dan downed the drink in three quick swigs and slid the empty glass back to her. "Don't dump out the ice or the lime, just add to it."

"Yes, sir!" she replied grabbing the glass and quickly making another drink. "This ones on me."

"I should hope so."

She raised one eyebrow and put the drink in front of Dan. "Are you busting my balls?"

"Obviously."

She smiled and walked to the other end of the bar to wait on some other customers.

Look back ... look back ... look back, Dan thought as he watched her ass wiggle away.

She looked back.

Yes! I still got it.

"What are you looking at, pal?" Red asked as he brought his hand down on Dan's shoulder startling him and making him spill his drink down the front of his shirt.

"Dammit!"

Red walked around behind the bar. "Pretty cute, isn't she?"

"I'll say. I bet she came with an extensive resume," Dan joked.

"She came with an extensive rack."

"Hey, I think that's sexual harassment."

"Is it? I thought I just couldn't say it to her face."

"Trust me; she knows you're thinking it."

Red leaned forward, resting his hairy forearms on the bar. "So, was the stakeout postponed until tonight?"

"Yeah, maybe we better head over there in a little while." Dan looked at the clock over the bar. It was nine-thirty. "One more for the road," he said, placing his glass at the edge of the bar.

Red made another drink and one for himself. As he handed the glass back to Dan the Dallas Cowboy barmaid appeared at Red's side. "Wasn't I doing a good enough job?" she asked smiling. She had a great smile, full lips, and thick eyebrows. Sexy, like Brook Shields' *used* to be.

"You were doing a *pretty* good job, but hey, practice makes perfect," Dan responded.

"You're terrible," she said, slapping Dan's arm.

"Carla, this is Dan Coast. Dan, this is Carla something," Red said.

Carla stuck out her hand. "Carla Lintz. It's nice to meet you."

Dan took her hand; it was small, soft, and warm. "Nice to meet you too."

Red grinned and jerked his head at Dan. "Dan here is a private investigator."

"Oh, really? My father is a cop in South Carolina."

Dan shook his head. "He's joking; I'm not really a private investigator."

Red kept going. "Dan's having a Christmas party tomorrow night. He was just asking me if you had tomorrow night off. He was wondering if you wanted to stop by for a drink. I told him the bar was closed tomorrow night."

Dan stared at Red; he could feel his face flush. He felt like he was in seventh grade again and his buddy Joe was asking a girl he liked out for him. As he recalled, she had turned him down, He never got over the mortification.

"Does he always get your dates for you?" Carla asked.

"No, sometimes I just slide a note to a girl that says *Do you like me? Check yes or no*."

Carla laughed. "I would love to come. What time?"

"Seven."

Dan felt something move in his pants. Luckily it was his cell phone vibrating. He pulled it from his pocket and looked at the screen and then at Red. "It's surfer dude." He hit the green icon. "Aloha, dude."

"Yo, Coast, you gotta get over here," Skip whispered. "These two dudes showed up in a FedEx van and put about ten packages in the marine store. Then when those dudes left, Ivan Drago and the little dark dude showed up in a UPS van. They're in the store right now."

Dan set his drink down. "We'll be right there. Stay out of sight."

Chapter Forty-One

Dan and Red sped along Flagler Avenue. When they came to the Mobil station Dan took a hard right into the parking lot and screeched into the first space he came to. Dan grabbed his pistol out of the glove box and the two men quickly jumped from the car and ran through the parking lot toward Riviera Avenue. Dan glanced through the windows of the gas station as they ran past; there was no sign of Skip, or Max Drescher for that matter. The older gentleman who was behind the counter didn't notice them as they ran by.

Dan reached the corner of the Mobil station first and slowed to a cautious walk, Red followed suit. When the two men got to the fence that bordered Flagler Marine, they stopped and took in their surroundings.

"Any sign of Skip?" Dan asked.

"No, but we ran right by his car," Red answered.

"Dammit, I told him to stay out of sight!"

Dan jumped up on the chain link fence and swung his leg over, dropping to the other side. Red flipped up the lock, opened the gate and walked through.

"Why do you assume everything is locked?" Red asked.

"Shut up!" Dan replied. He was halfway to the steps that led to the loading dock and the back door of the store. Red joined him at the top of the stairs.

Dan put his face close to the glass to look inside. "If the green light is blinking, does that mean the alarm is on or off?"

"Only one way to find out," Red said, pulling the door open. "See, unlocked."

Dan rolled his eyes, removed his gun from his waistband and quietly followed Red through the door.

Red stopped. "Did you hear that?"

"Hear what?" Dan whispered.

"It sounded like paper tearing."

Dan started to tell Red that it was just his imagination, but then he heard it too. Both men dropped to their knees behind steel shelving loaded with anti-freeze. Dan put his index finger to his lips. Red pointed to the other side of the room, then to his eyes, then his ear, and then swung his arm in a throwing motion.

Dan whispered, "I have no idea what that means."

"You go around the shelves that way," Red whispered. "I'll throw something in the opposite direction to distract 'em. When they look that way, you jump 'em."

"How will I know they're looking in that direction?"

"I'm sure they will, wouldn't you?"

"I might just think someone was trying to get me to look in that direction."

"That's because you have to question everything. Trust me; they'll look in the direction of the noise."

"Trust me, he says," Dan grumbled as he made his way to the end of the shelving.

Red grabbed a small twelve-volt battery off the shelf and heaved it in the opposite direction. Dan ran around to the other aisle, gun drawn.

"Yo, Coast! What took you dudes so long?" Skip stood in front of a long metal table tearing open a package wrapped in brown paper. "Look at all this coke, dude!"

Dan joined Skip at the table as Red walked down the aisle.

"That's a lot of coke," Dan commented.

"Is yur dad here, dude?"

"No," Dan said pointing at Red. "Skip, Red. Red, Skip."

Skip thrust his hand at Red. "It's a pleasure to make your acquaintance, Red. Any friend of Coast's is a friend of mine."

Red shook his hand. "That's good to know, Skip."

"Fourteen bags of this shit," Dan said.

"There was a lot more than this, dude. The two guys in that UPS truck took about ten of 'em out of here."

"So let me get this straight," Dan said, scratching his head. "A FedEx truck delivered some coke and then a UPS truck came and picked it up?"

Skip shook his head. "Exactamundo, dude."

"What can Brown do for you?" Red quipped.

Skip laughed. "Ha, just like the commercials. Good one, Red Man."

Red turned to Dan. "Do you think it's time to call the cops?"

"I say we take all this blow, wait to see who wants it back, and then we trade it for that old dude that owns this place," Skip suggested.

Dan and Red looked at each other. "Actually, that's a pretty good idea," Dan decided.

"Sounds good to me," Red agreed.

"Okay then, it's settled," Skip said. "Let's load this dope into my car and I'll stash it at my house."

"Um, I think it would be a better idea if we just hid it here in the building," Dan reasoned. "That way none of us gets caught with it. I doubt the cops would believe you were just holding it for a friend."

"Dan, the man with a plan!" Skip commented. He held up his hand for a high five. Dan did so half-heartedly.

"How about if we hide it up in the drop ceiling?" Red suggested.

"Good idea," Dan agreed, pointing to the other side of the room. "Skip, get that step ladder over there and meet me in the corner."

Skip ran to the other side of the store, grabbed the ladder, and joined Red and Dan. Dan unfolded the ladder and climbed to the top rung. He reached above his head, lifted a ceiling panel and slid it to the side. Skip handed Dan the packages of cocaine one at a time and Dan placed each one up into the ceiling.

Skip stood at the bottom of the ladder as Dan finished and slid the panel back into place. "Dude, it says here that you're not supposed to stand on the top rung. It says it's not a step."

Dan looked down at his helper. "Does it say anything about not being used to stash drugs in a ceiling?"

Skip put his head closer to the ladder. "Um …"

"Get out of the way!" Dan said, climbing down. "And put the ladder back where you got it."

Skip did as he was told and joined Dan and Red outside at the loading dock.

"Now listen," Dan said. "It seems like every time these guys show up it's about this same time of night, so I say we all go about our business and then meet back up here tomorrow night around eight-thirty."

"What about your Christmas party?" Red asked.

"Whoa!" Skip threw up his hands "You're having a Christmas party and you didn't invite me? Not cool, dude, not cool."

"Sorry, dude. Would you like to come to my Christmas party?"

"I accept your invitation, Dan, *Muchas gray suits*."

Dan rolled his eyes and turned back to Red. "The party starts at seven. We'll hang around for about an hour and a half, then we'll sneak out and come over here."

"Roger that, dude," Skip said as he pulled a small leather case from his pants pocket.

Dan and Red watched quietly as Skip slid two metal instruments that resembled dental tools, from the case and inserted them into the lock. He twisted them one way and then back the other. The lock clicked. When Skip turned around he saw the two men staring at him. "What, did you think those drug dealers just left the door unlocked?" he said, putting the case back in his pocket.

"I'm not even going to ask you why you carry around that case, Skip," said Dan.

Skip collapsed in hilarity. "Ha-ha, it's prob'ly best that you don't, dude!"

All three men walked to the fence, climbed over, and

made their way back to the gas station parking lot. Skip sped off in one direction and Dan and Red in the other.

Dan had only made it a few blocks down Flagler when his phone began to ring. He answered it.

"Dude," came the voice from the other end. "Three things: Is this thing tomorrow night formal? Should I bring something? And can I bring a date?"

Chapter Forty-Two

Dan was beginning to get used to waking up in the morning with the wonderful aroma of bacon wafting through the house. He lay in his bed on his back staring up at the slowly spinning blades of the ceiling fan and listening to his mother and father playfully bicker. It was never the bickering of people who couldn't stand each other, but rather of two people who had loved each other for a long time. Dan had heard his parents good-natured banter his whole life, and hearing it now made him feel like he was home. He smiled.

Swinging his legs over the side of the bed, he stood and walked shirtless to the bathroom. The window in the bathroom was open and once again he could hear Christmas music coming from Bev's house. Today it didn't seem to bother him as much. With his morning leak out of the way, he pulled on a T-shirt and headed for the kitchen.

"Hey, sleepyhead, I didn't think you were gonna get out of bed this morning!" his mom greeted him. "It's almost ten o'clock."

Dan stretched his arms over his head and groaned. "I

slept great last night," he said. "That's good, dear. Scrambled or fried?" Peg asked.

"Scrambled, thanks," Dan answered. He took a coffee cup from the cabinet and poured himself a cup of coffee. "Where's Dad?"

"Where do you think?" She nodded toward the backyard as she cracked the eggs.

Dan sipped his coffee as he stood in front of the screen door, watching his father fill in the crossword puzzle. Buddy lay at the bottom of the steps next to his water dish. Dan turned and went to the dining room table to drink his coffee and read the sections of the paper that his father had left behind.

"Here ya go, Danny," Peg said as she sat his plate in front of him.

"Thanks, Mom, looks great." Dan held the paper at arm's length as he read about the owner of a Napa Auto Parts store in Arcadia who had been missing for a week. He was a widower and his children lived up north. Neighbors noticed something was wrong when newspapers started piling up outside the man's home.

"Arms getting too short?" Peg asked.

"What?"

"You're holding that newspaper pretty far away from your face. Maybe you need glasses."

"I can see just fine, Mother."

"You're in your forties now. You father started wearing glasses when he was thirty-nine, I've worn them since I was a kid. Maybe it's time to get your eyes checked."

"Maybe it's time for you to drop it," Dan suggested.

"I'm just saying."

"Just don't."

Peg got up from the table and went to the back door. "More coffee, Gene?"

"Yup," he yelled back.

Peg picked up the pot and walked out the back door.

Good, go bug him for a while, Dan thought.

Dan sat and flipped through the paper until he came to the comics. He was about half-way down the page when there was a knock at the door. Dan glanced up through the open front door and saw a deliveryman in a brown button-up shirt and brown shorts. Parked in the street behind him was a UPS van. Dan felt the hair on the back of his neck stand up. *Shit, how did they find me?* he wondered. "Can I help you?" he called through the screen door. He thought about his gun in the glove compartment.

The man's eyes went to the electronic clipboard in his right hand. "I've got a delivery for Dan Coast."

"From who?" Dan asked, stalling. He wondered if they had found the drugs in the ceiling. He wondered if his parents were safe outback or if someone else had gone around to the back door. Dan wished his gun was in his waistband now.

"Sure you got the right address?"

The man looked back at his clipboard. "No doubt about it, sir. Package is from Custom Outdoor," he responded.

Dan relaxed. *Oh yeah, the Christmas present*, he remembered. He went to the door and signed for his package. His hand was shaky as he signed.

"You okay?" the driver asked.

"Yeah, I thought you were someone else."

The deliveryman shrugged his shoulders. "Happy

Holiday, sir," he said.

"What's wrong with Merry Christmas?" Dan said.

"Nothing, sir. We're just not supposed to say it. Company policy.

Goddamn political correctness. "Well, Merry Christmas to you, anyway."

"Thanks, sir. You have a good one."

"That's what I've been told, "Dan said automatically. Scowling, the driver returned to his van.

Dan dragged the box into the living room and began ripping it open.

"Watcha got there, Sonny," Gene asked as he walked into the room.

"It's a gift for that kid over on Sky View."

Dan pulled a small green bicycle from the cardboard box and set it on the floor beside him.

"A bike?" Gene questioned.

"That's an odd-looking bike," Peg added.

"It's a custom bike, made just for little people." Dan straddled the bike. "See, the bar in the middle is down farther so his feet can reach the ground, and the seat and handlebars are closer together."

"That's great, Sonny, the kids gonna love it," Gene said.

Peg walked over and put her hand on her son's back. "That's a nice thing to do, Danny."

"Yeah, well, the kid was riding around on a girl's bike that had been left at the house. I just thought this might work out a little better for him." Dan swung his leg off of the bike and rolled it over by the Christmas tree. "I'll bring it over tomorrow."

When Dan had parked the bike he noticed there were four or five gifts that had been placed under the tree. *Crap, I better get to the mall,* he thought.

Chapter Forty-Three

It was after two o'clock by the time Dan persuaded his friend Red to accompany him to the mall. He wasn't hard to convince, the mention of a free lunch was all it took. Dan knew he had better spring for lunch before the Christmas shopping began or that's all he would hear about until that time.

Dan wanted to grab a quick pizza, but Red had his heart set on TGI Fridays, so TGI Fridays it was. They both had entrees from the Jack Daniel's menu. Dan ruefully observed that not only did he like to drink liquor, now he liked to eat it, too.

After lunch was out of the way the shopping frenzy began. Dan chose to start at Kmart. He figured if they didn't sell it at K-Mart then his parents didn't need it.

"Who all are you buying for?" Red asked.

"My mother and father," Dan answered.

"That's it?"

"Who else is there?"

"Nobody, I guess."

Dan went up one aisle and down the other with Red quietly trailing along. They looked at tools; they looked at cook wear. "I don't know what to get them," Dan concluded. "Maybe a gift card or something."

"Your parents come all the way down here for Christmas and all you're going to get them is a gift card?"

"What's wrong with that? That's what you get for somebody who has everything: a gift card."

Red rolled his eyes. "Why dontcha get your dad some tools or something."

"If he wants a tool he buys it himself. And what do you mean they came all the way down here for Christmas? You're the one that *called* them down here."

Red tried to play dumb. "Whaaaat?"

"Bev let it slip; I know the whole story, pal."

"Well, what did you expect me to do? Every year you go into hiding and, start drinking way too much … and this year it started much sooner than usual. We all worry about you. So I called them. Big deal."

"Don't worry about me," Dan said coolly as he turned and started back down the aisle.

"You should buy them a house down here."

"Yeah that's *all* I need. I don't mind seeing them for a day or two, but if they were here for a whole winter I would probably put a bullet in my head."

"Yeah, I guess you're right. It's too bad you can't control when they get here and when they leave," Red said.

A light went on in Dan's head and he spun around. "Maybe I can. Come on, let's get out of here! I've got an idea for the perfect Christmas gift for Mom and Dad."

Chapter Forty-Four

The Christmas party wasn't supposed to start until seven. At six forty-five Dan was in his room buttoning his shirt when he heard the first knock at the door. When he heard the deep, froggy voice that was drowning out Perry Como's rendition of "I'll Be Home For Christmas," he knew it was Red. *Always the first one to arrive at a party, and always the last one to leave*, Dan thought, and smiled.

As Dan exited the hall into the dining room Mrs. McGee was coming through the door followed by Bev. Before the door could be shut Skip entered with his date. Dan, Red, and Gene's eyes bugged out of their heads. Skip's date looked like, walked like, and dressed like a Victoria's Secret model. She was a statuesque brunette in a sheer black button-up top that someone had forgotten to button, not that the men minded. The delectable breasts spilling out of the barely there black lace bra had them praising God for clearly working overtime on this beauteous amazon. She had on a black mini skirt that knew exactly where her butt cheeks stopped and her long muscular legs began. Her lustrous hair hung mid-way down her back and was tucked back behind her ears, revealing little green Christmas bulbs that dangled from each lobe. They flashed rhythmically, bringing out the green in the superwoman's eyes.

Red jabbed Dan in the ribs. "Is this what they mean by, *there's someone for everyone*?"

"Maybe, but I think Skip got someone else's."

Skip introduced his lady as Tiffany, and she soon excused herself to mingle.

"Close your mouth, Gene," Peg said as she walked from the kitchen with a large plastic bowl of potato chips. "You act like you've never seen a pair of tits before."

"I've never seen any like *that*," Gene whispered to Dan and Red.

The front door was open, and Dan spied Carla Lintz, rapping on the door jamb. Dan almost mowed his mother down trying to get to the door first. "Hey, thanks for coming, Carla," he said as he motioned her into the house.

Dan introduced Carla to his mother and father and then to Bev. Dan looked around his house as the Christmas music played and everyone chatted. His house had never been this full before, and it sure as hell had never been this happy before. He pulled his cell phone from his pocket and looked at the time; he wished he didn't have to leave.

Around eight-thirty there was another knock at the door; it was Michael from the restaurant. "Daniel, oh Daniel!" he called out as he swished across the floor, dragging an older man behind him. "Daniel, this is my boyfriend Scott. Scott this is my very dear friend Daniel. He's a private detective, just like Magnum P.I."

"And just as good-looking," Scott cooed.

Michael slapped his partner on the arm. "You're terrible, Scott! Don't you be looking at anyone other than me tonight, you slut. Now get me a drink, Daniel, you're a horrible host. I'm just joshing you, silly." Michael pinched his cheek and tittered.

Dan somehow managed a grin and joined his father at the bar. "Did you invite Michael?"

"Yeah," Gene responded, dropping ice into his glass. "Your mother and I had lunch where he was working the other day. I figured the more the merrier."

"Oh, he's merry, all right," Dan commented. "Like an elf."

At nine o'clock Skip and Red joined Dan in the kitchen. "It's about time to go," Red pointed out.

"We'll sneak out the back door," Dan suggested. "Let me go in first and tell my dad to cover for us."

Dan returned to the party and whispered into his father's ear. Gene nodded. Then Dan pulled Carla aside and told her he would be back as soon as he could, and that he hoped she would still be here when he got back. She smiled and explained, with a whisper in his ear, that it would be in his best interest if he returned promptly. He felt something move in his pants again: this time it was not his phone.

As Dan made his way back to the kitchen Michael grabbed his arm. "Daniel, can I talk to you for a minute?"

"Uh … I gotta make a quick run to the store," Dan responded.

"It's kind of important, Daniel."

Dan saw the look of concern in Michael's eyes. "What's the matter?"

"Well, I know you have this whole private eye thing you do and my father has this friend, Mr. Norton, that's been missing for a few days. He called the police yesterday, but because he's not a family member, they didn't pay him much attention. They gave him some story about not looking into missing persons for twenty-four hours or some such nonsense."

"Exactly how long has he been missing?"

"Well, my father hasn't seen him in four or five days. His store was closed yesterday and today and when my dad went by his house he didn't answer the door. I told my father about you and I said I would ask you if you would look around the store and maybe drive by his house."

"Sure, I can do that for your dad, Michael. Where is his store?"

"He owns Flagler Marine."

"Flagler Marine?"

"Yes, I believe it's a boat parts store or some such silly thing."

Dan turned to see Red and Skip listening in. "Where does he live?"

"Right near his store, at the corner of Riviera Drive and Eleventh Street."

Dan turned to Skip. "When that third guy came back to the store the other night, you said he was a big dude. Did you mean big and muscular?"

Skip shook his head. "No way, Jose. This guy was a big fat dude. He looked kinda like a big dude on a cop show my dad used to watch."

"*Jake and the Fat Man?*" Dan asked.

"No, dude, that wasn't it."

"*Cannon?*" Red suggested.

"That's the guy, Red Man! My dad used to groove out on that show all the time."

"Same guy in both shows," Dan said, showing off his encyclopedic TV knowledge. "William Conrad."

"Baa, Baa, Black Sheep," Gene yelled from the other room.

"That was *Robert* Conrad, Dad." He turned to Red and Skip. "Come on, guys. Let's split."

"Hey, who's gonna look after Tiffany?" Skip asked.

I will," said Gene, emerging from the other room with Tiffany on his arm.

Chapter Forty-Five

Dan, Red, and Skip slipped out the back door with the party still in full swing. Red took a right onto Eleventh Street and then another quick right into a vacant lot stopping his Volkswagen Bug and turning off the engine behind some trees. The intrepid trio exited the car and stood next to the street looking toward old man Norton's house. The three windows facing Eleventh Street were lit. The Russian was walking back and forth in the yard, smoking a cigarette.

"Looks like Drago is guarding the place," Skip offered.

"When he walks around the other side of the house we'll run up to the fence and see if we can get a better look," Dan said.

The three watched as the big Russian rounded the corner. "Now," Dan whispered.

They ran to the three-foot cement fence and crouched behind it just as Drago came back around the house. He took one last long drag on his cigarette, flicked it into the street, and went in through the side door.

"Me and Red are gonna jump the fence and see if we can get a look in one of the windows," Dan said to Skip. "You stay here. If anything goes wrong, just call 911; tell them you heard gunshots. And don't ask me the number for 911!"

Skip did his Spicoli laugh and shushed himself. "Ha-ha. Good one, dude."

Dan yanked his pistol from his waistband, ejected the magazine from the grip, and looked at the bullets. Then he jammed the magazine back into place with the palm of his hand.

"What was that for?" Red asked.

"I have no idea, but they always do it on TV."

"Maybe they're scared and they're just trying to stall," Skip said, pulling a .38 from the holster clipped to his belt. Red and Dan looked at him with some incredulity. This goofy surfer dude was full of surprises.

"Why do you carry a lock picking kit and a gun?" Dan asked.

Skip laughed raucously and shushed himself again. "Don't ask, don't tell, dude!"

"So, I'm the only one without a gun? That's just great!" Red complained.

"Come on," Dan said, leaping over the fence.

Red followed and they ran up to the closest window and peeked inside. It was a jalousie window with louvers operated by a crank mechanism. The louvers were open, and they could hear snatches of dialogue from within. The Russian and the short dark-skinned man sat at the dining room table playing cards. Milton Guff, if that was his real name, stood in front of the stove stirring something in a large stainless steel pot. Red and Dan squatted back down.

"No sign of Norton," Dan said.

Red nodded. "Probably tied up in one of the bedrooms."

"If he's here at all."

"How should we go about this?"

"I'm open to any suggestions."

"Maybe it's time to call the cops?"

"What fun would that be?" Dan grinned. "Come on."

The two men ran around to the side of the house to the garage and peeked through the garage door. Inside the garage was a distinctive brown van. "UPS," Dan whispered.

As quietly as possible, the two men made their way back to the front of the house. Dan reached down and picked up a large white-painted rock from a flower-bed border and handed it to Red.

"I'm gonna put Skip on the other side of the house and then call 911," said Dan. "When you hear me whistle, throw this rock through that window." He pointed at the large window in the front of the house. "And then get back over the fence. Got it? And don't say roger that, dude."

Red grinned. "Got it."

Dan left Red and, hunching over, ran back around the house, back to Skip, who was waiting on the other side of the fence. "Skip, come with me!" he beckoned.

Skip followed Dan back to window, where the men could be seen playing cards and cooking dinner. They squatted beneath the window. "You stay here by this window," said Dan. "Red is going to throw a rock through the front window. When he does, these guys will run out front to see what's going on. I'll go through the side door and look for Norton. If anyone comes back through the kitchen, you shoot."

"Roger that, dude."

Dan pulled out his cell phone, called 911, and set his phone on the ground. "Ready?" he asked Skip.

"I was born ready, dude! Let's kick some ace."

Dan whistled … and nothing. He and Skip looked at each other. Dan whistled again. The sound of breaking glass that they had expected to hear didn't come.

Skip rose up and peered inside the house. "Um, dude, you might want to see this."

Dan put his head next to Skips and looked in. Standing in the middle of the kitchen was Red. His hands were in the air and the Russian's gun was shoved in his back.

"Son of a bitch," Dan whispered.

They could hear Drago's voice through the jalousie windows. "I went out the front door to have another smoke and this asshole was standing in the front yard with a rock in his hand."

"I know this guy," Milton said. "Him and another guy was here asking questions the day you shot that guy." Milton pulled a pistol from a shoulder holster and shoved the barrel against Red's temple. "Where's your nosey friend?"

Red said, "I'm here by myself. He went for the cops."

"Did he, now?" Milton responded smashing the gun butt down on Red's skull, knocking him to the floor.

Dan could see the stream of blood coming from Red's head. Milton shoved the barrel into the back of Red's head. "If you're listening to me," he yelled, "you have five seconds to come in here or I re-stain the floor with his brains. One … two … three."

Milton pulled the hammer back on the gun. Dan could

hear it click into place.

"Four …"

"Okay!" Dan hollered. "I'm coming in." Dan put his gun in the back of his waistband. "Stay close but be inconspicuous. Some serious shit's about to go down," he whispered to Skip.

Dan opened the side door and went into the kitchen.

Red was on his knees, blood streaming down his face. "Sorry, Dan," he said.

"No sweat, friend," he said to Red, and turned to face Milton. "Where's Norton?" Dan asked.

"You're one inquisitive bastard, aren't you?" Milton said.

"So I've been told." Dan paused. He needed to keep the thugs distracted so they wouldn't think of frisking him for weapons. "Uh, by the way, Milton …"

"Yes?"

"Thanks for wearing a shirt today."

Red guffawed. The smaller man, who was busy screwing a silencer on his pistol, paused to kick him in the gut.

"You want me to bring them in the bedroom and put one in their skulls, boss?" he asked.

"Patience, Lenny, patience," Milton answered. He looked at Dan. "Your friend here didn't have a gun. Do you?"

Dan didn't miss a beat. "We're just your friendly neighborhood vigilantes of justice. We fight crime with our wits, not guns. But the cops are on their way, and they've got plenty of guns."

"It doesn't matter. You'll both be dead when they get

here, and we'll be long gone." Milton turned to the Russian. "Start loading the van, Steven, we're done here."

Steven? Dan mused. *A helluva American-as-apple-pie name for a Russkie.*

He regarded Milton. If he was like the heavies from every TV show and spy flick he'd ever seen, Milton was a vainglorious crook who wouldn't be able to resist launching into a longwinded account of his scheme for the edification of his soon-to-die captives. That would buy him more time. Maybe he could even manage to pull his own gun while Milton ran off at the mouth. Maybe skip would burst in like the cavalry. Maybe monkeys would fly out of his ass.

"Tell me, Milton," he began, what exactly *were* you doing here?"

Milton laughed. "Dan, is it? This isn't the end of a Bond film or some crappy mystery novel. I'm not going to stand here and explain everything to you in detail while you stall for time. There's not going to be some glorious shoot out ending in the death of all the bad guys while the good guys high-five over their dead bodies. That's not the way it works in the real world."

So much for that idea, Dan thought, but tried again anyway. "But, why did you tell us about the black car, and hearing the gunshot before you saw the truck? It doesn't make sense, Milton. You had already paid Max to lie about it."

"I didn't pay anybody," Milton responded, motioning toward Lenny. "These two morons did and neglected to inform me. Besides who would have thought you two morons would have put it all together anyway?" Milton laughed out loud. "When you think about it, you two didn't even solve this little caper, I solved it for you."

Milton returned his own gun to his shoulder holster

and held out his flabby paw for Lenny's. "I do so hate the sound of loud gunfire, don't you, Dan? It sounds so … final."

Dan said nothing. He scanned the jalousie window for some sign of Skip. *Shit, not there. Shouldn't have told him to be inconspicuous. He probably went for a dictionary to look it up.* Red braced himself and prayed.

"The good guys rarely win, Dan."

Milton raised Lenny's gun to the back of Red's head.

Dan inched his hand to his waistband.

Bang!

A round from Skips .38 shattered the window and lodged in the yellow-stucco wall behind Lenny. Milton turned his bulk toward the clatter as Dan jerked his gun from his waistband and fired a shot into the fat man's chest. Instinctively Lenny reached for his empty holster. Dan put two bullets into Lenny's torso, driving him backwards and onto the table. Playing cards flew from the table and scattered to the floor.

Milton, leaning against the cabinets, tried to raise the gun but it slipped from his fingers and hit the floor near Red. Red picked it up and quickly got to his feet. He pointed the gun at Lenny and then at Milton.

"Don't move!" came the Russian's voice from the kitchen doorway. "Drop the gu—"

A bullet from Skip's pistol entered his back and burst through the front of his shirt, bringing with it blood, flesh, and bone. He looked down disbelievingly at the growing bloodstain on his chest, dropped to his knees, and finally crashed face-first onto the old wooden floor.

Sirens screamed in the distance. Dan watched as Red raised his gun and pointed it at Milton's face. "Did you eat that donut in Phil's truck, you fat bastard?"

Milton's face had grown pale as the life left his body. He tried to steady himself. His knees buckled and he hit the floor with a *thunk* that shook the entire house.

The bigger they are the harder they fall, Dan thought.

Skip stood in the kitchen doorway, the dead Russian at his feet. "Sorry I didn't show up sooner, dudes," he said cheerfully, "but I hadda take a leak."

"You had to take a leak!" Red was apoplectic. "I could have been kil—"

"Later, Red," said Dan. "I'm just glad we brought you along, Skip."

"No problem. Hey, dudes, waddabout Norton?"

The trio went down the hallway to the bedroom and Dan opened the door. Tied up and with duct tape stretched across his mouth, but very much alive, was Mr. Norton. As gingerly as he could, Dan pulled the tape off of his mouth. "Are you okay?" Dan asked.

Norton nodded his head yes.

The sirens grew closer.

Red looked at the time on his cell phone. "Ten-thirty! We've got a party to get back to."

Dan helped Norton back to the kitchen and sat him in a chair.

Skip looked at the three dead bodies on the floor and raised his hand in the air. "Whoa, nice tally! High five, dudes!"

This time Dan was only too happy to oblige.

Chapter Forty-Six

It was a little after ten o'clock on Christmas morning before Gene picked up his son and his friends from the police station after a long night of questioning.

Skip's girlfriend, leaning against her crimson red BMW 3 series 328i convertible, patiently waited for his release. When she saw him she waved and smiled a megawatt smile that would light up a roadway. She was wearing faded denim short shorts and a black sports bra that she had obviously washed in very hot water and left in the dryer just a little bit too long. On her feet were white sneakers, no socks.

"Please, please, tell me, Skip, old buddy," Red implored, "what have you got that I ain't got?"

Skip looked confused. "I don't getcha, Red Man."

"Never mind."

Skip shuffled to the car. Dan, Red, and Gene watched as Skip's girlfriend opened the door for him, closed it after he got in, walked around to the driver's side, got in, and drove away.

Coasts of Christmas Past

"He must be hung like a goddamn horse," Gene commented.

"Yeah, that must be it," Red sighed.

The three men climbed into Gene's rental car and headed for home with more questions than answers. They had found out who shot Phil, and that's what April had asked them to find out, so in a way it was mission accomplished.

It would be another four or five weeks before Dan and Red would get all the answers in the form of a story in the *Key West Citizen.* The story would tell about an FBI and DEA investigation into a ring of drug dealers who targeted single business owners with little or no immediate family. They would take the owner captive, close down his business for a few weeks, and then run their drug shipments through the businesses with a fake fleet of UPS and FedEx vans. Over thirty arrests were made and eleven small business owners were found murdered in their homes or stores during the investigation, and over forty million dollars in cocaine was seized. For their own safety, Dan, Red, and Skip's names were never mentioned in the story.

Phil, the tough old buzzard that he was, pulled through, and the doctors said he could resume being a royal pain in April's ass in no time.

*****

In the meantime, on that sunny Christmas morning in Key West, Dan piled out of his father's Focus and stood shamefacedly before his mother in the living room.

"You're late," Peg joked. "The party ended around midnight."

Dan hugged his mother. "Sorry, Mom, maybe next year."

"Next year?"

"Yeah," Dan said, pulling an envelope from the branches of the Christmas tree and handing it to his mother. "Here, I got this for you and Dad."

Peg opened the envelope and removed the papers inside. "What is this?"

"I went to the travel agency and got you and Dad a cruise. It's for next Christmas time. The ship leaves out of New York Harbor and stops here in Key West for a day before going on to the Bahamas."

Peg hugged her son. "Thanks, Danny, that's the most wonderful gift you could have given us."

Peg stuffed the paperwork back into the envelope, handed it to Gene, and returned to her post-Christmas party clean-up.

Gene winked at his son. "One day in Key West, huh?"

Dan returned to the tree and proceeded to roll the bicycle out the front door. "I got a quick errand to run, Dad."

Dan loaded the bike into the passenger seat of his car and drove over to Sky View Street. It was a beautiful morning, not a cloud in the sky. The voice on the radio said it was seventy-one degrees today in Key West with a slight breeze out of the south, and then Jimmy Buffett began singing "A Sailor's Christmas." *God, I love that song*! He sang along at the top of his lungs.

Dan pulled to the curb in front of Noah's house and parked. Leaving the engine running, he removed the bike, rolled it up the sidewalk, and set it on the front porch. He kicked down the kickstand and knocked on the door. He waited a few seconds and knocked again. Behind him he heard a screen door slam and saw Mrs. Fields crossing the street.

"Good morning! Merry Christmas!" Dan called out, grinning ear to ear.

When Mrs. Fields got to the other side of the street her drawn little face was as sour as ever. But there was something new there, a deep sadness in her eyes.

Dan was feeling too good to notice. "I got Noah a little something for Christmas!" he said cheerily, pointing at the bike. "They must not be home."

Mrs. Fields looked at the small green bike and a tear slowly made its way down her cheek. "Mr. Coast, Noah's gone."

The smile left Dan's face. "Gone? Gone where? What do you mean?"

"He passed away yesterday afternoon, Mr. Coast. It was his heart."

Dan didn't say a word. He picked up the bike, put it back in the car, and drove away. He took a right off of Atlantic Boulevard on to Bertha Street. When he got to the end of Bertha he pulled to the side of the road and got out of his car. Dan reached under his front seat and grabbed his bottle of tequila in one hand and picked up the bike with the other. Dan walked to the edge of the sidewalk and stood behind the three-foot concrete wall that separated the land from the sea. He set the bike down, opened the bottle, and took a long drink. Setting the bottle on the cement wall, he picked up the bike in both hands, and, as hard as he could, threw it into the ocean.

Dan stood staring quietly out at the horizon as he finished his bottle of tequila.

The End

Don't miss Rodney Riesel's most recent exciting book.

Who is he?
Why is he here?
Where is he from?

The Man in Room Number Four

ALSO BY RODNEY RIESEL

Sleeping Dogs Lie
From the Tales of Dan Coast

A mystery set in the Florida Keys follows Dan Coast, an unlicensed private detective of sorts, as he is hired to find the missing boyfriend of a woman who herself soon ends up missing. When someone from the woman's past unexpectedly shows up at Dan's home, with a story of faked deaths and missing life insurance money; Dan along with his sidekick Red set out to find the money, and the woman.

ISBN: 978-0-9883503-0-4

Ocean Floors
From the Tales of Dan Coast

The second installment in the Dan Coast series, Ocean Floors, is a tale of mystery and possible romance when a chance meeting with a beautiful young woman leads Dan and his trusted sidekick Red down a road of murder and kidnapping. Join Dan and Red as they try to solve the murder while searching for a missing friend.

ISBN: 978-0-9894877-0-2

Impaled
An Adirondack Short Story

Eric Stone is an investigator with The Town of Webb Police Department. Chuck Little is Head Ranger at the Nick's Lake campground. An unlikely duo, together they work to solve a murder that mimics a spree of gruesome murders taking place years earlier. Is it a copycat, or has the murderer resurfaced after all of these years? Join Stone and Little as they piece together the clues to solve this mystery taking place in the small village of Old Forge in the Adirondack Mountains.

North Murder Beach
A Jake Stellar Novel

The first installment of the story of North Myrtle Beach police detective, Jake Stellar. The spring bike rallies have ended, the spring breakers have all gone back to school, and the summer tourist season is a few weeks away. What better time for a police officer to take a nice quiet relaxing week off from work? That's what Jake Stellar had in mind. That is until someone from his past resurfaces to remind him of a terrible secret he has spent years trying to forget. In North Murder Beach, a story of revenge, Jake is unwillingly and violently forced to confront his secret from his past.

ISBN: 978-0-9894877-1-9